# a very, very bad thing

# a

# very,

# very

# bad

# thing

## jeffery self

Library of Congress Cataloging-in-Publication Data available

ISBN 978-1-338-11840-7

10 9 8 7 6 5 4 3 2 1          17 18 19 20 21

Printed in the U.S.A.  23
First edition, November 2017
Book design by Carol Ly and Baily Crawford

*To anyone who needs to hear to it:*

*You are not alone.*

a very, very bad thing

# NOW

I AM NOT A BAD person. I'm not a great person either, but not bad. No matter how it might seem, no matter what I did.

Stupid? Yes.

Desperate? Yes.

Completely and totally lost beyond all belief? Abso-damn-lutely.

But not a bad person.

I'm someone who wanted to make a difference. I'm a nobody who wanted to be a somebody.

Up until a few months ago I was just another snarky gay kid from Winston-Salem, North Carolina, watching life through the disconnected Instagram filter of my generation and judging every minute of it. Now I'm in New York City, safely tucked away into yet another dressing room with my name written across the door in bold, joyous letters—the kind of happy letters that should never be associated with the kind of cause we're here to shed light upon. (*Shedding light* is something I've been asked to do a lot in these past few months, and I'm still not sure what the hell it even means.)

I can hear the crowd of three hundred or so very rich people cheering. Some D-list pop star whose name I can't remember and who recently came out of the closet the day his new album dropped (zero coincidence, I'm *sure*) is singing a song that sounds like a thousand other pop songs I've heard before.

*"Love me for who I am . . . and for who you are . . . and for who we all are and for who they are,"* he sings, including just about everything in his lyrics except a rhyme scheme.

I try not to judge this pop star, but it's hard. Judging pop stars is a part of my DNA, like having green eyes or preferring bubble baths over showers.

There's a rundown order taped to the door listing all of the evening's performers and speakers. One more singer, the cast of Broadway's *Wicked*, and three more speeches before I have to go out and accept the award. Roughly thirty minutes for me to change my mind, to chicken out and allow this whole charade to continue.

I should not be here. I know that now and I knew it before, but I wasn't paying attention. I was so caught up in my anger, in my rage to fix everything. There was too much going on to pay attention until I woke up from the nightmare and realized it was too late. For the first time in my life I've been given something to wake up for, something to accomplish, a reason, a some-thing, a *purpose*. Besides getting the ability to fly or winning a lifetime supply of freshly baked blueberry scones, discovering your purpose in life is one of the greatest things that can happen to a human being. Or so that's what every teacher, book, movie, television show, motivational speaker, and Bono says.

In the past few months, I have attended so many events like this one. I am as over it as Britney Spears has been on every award show she's performed on since 2004. I can't possibly stand in front of another step and repeat, smiling and claiming that "it gets better." I mean, does it? Sure, I've been flown around the country, getting to rub elbows with the most famous gay people in the world. Sure, everyone calls me a trailblazer. Sure, I saved our house. Sure, I've been interviewed by *Time* and CNN and even got to high-five Kathie Lee Gifford on live television . . . but none of it has been real or earned or right. I have *done* something. I have become a somebody, but by doing so I feel more like a nobody than ever before. So . . . did it get better?

Maybe for me. Not for Christopher.

But I can't think about Christopher.

Except I always think about Christopher.

If he asked me, "What are you doing here?" would I even have an answer other than "I have absolutely no freaking clue"?


Harrison, my manager and media consultant (whatever *that* means), has gone out to complain to someone about there being no Fiji Water in my dressing room. According to Harrison, this is a very big deal. I couldn't care less—I'll drink any water you put in front of me as long as it's clear and doesn't have fish swimming in it. Regardless, it's nice to be alone for a moment.

Harrison has left me with the speech I'm to give, accepting my Leading Change Award. Harrison wrote it for me—it's a good speech, because despite being a genuine mess, Harrison is a good writer. Apparently he used to write speeches for important people like senators and Susan Sarandon. According to Harrison and the *New York Times*, I am now one of these important people. This is the kind of speech that will be interrupted countless times for applause and cheering—the moments are literally written in. This is the kind of speech that will inevitably go online and be posted within hours on every gay blog and liberal media outlet celebrating how much of a hero I am.

*Hero* used to mean very little to me, aside from being a way to describe the hot spandex-clad dudes in comic book movies or Oprah. Nowadays, it's a word I hear a lot.

No one but my best friend, Audrey, knows what's folded up in my pocket, what I've scribbled down on a ripped-out page from my journal. What I stayed up all night last night writing when the guilt got too overwhelming to even consider sleep as an option.

I stare at myself in the mirror. I look way better than I did before all this happened. I'm in a fancy suit, I've got an expensive haircut, and I'm wearing just enough stage makeup to make me look pretty yet still handsome. The baby fat that kept my face in a shape far closer to circular than I've ever been happy about is gone. Harrison has forced me to work out with a personal trainer (a legitimate monster of a woman named Kimberly) and kept me away from carbs as if they were some kind of poison.

I don't recognize myself at all.

I haven't in a very long time.

There's a knock on my dressing room door. "Come in," I say as a stage manager pokes her head in.

"You've got roughly twenty minutes, Marley," she tells me.

I thank her as she closes the door. I take a deep breath.

"You can do this," I say to myself so quietly that I wonder if it's inside my head. "It's going to be okay."

I can't get his face out of my head. Not from that awful night, but from the day in September when I saw him for the very first time and our story didn't have an ending yet.

I've never been one to buy into sappy things like "kismet" or "fate," but for the millisecond when I first laid eyes on Christopher, I did.

# MONDAY, SEPTEMBER 3,
# 8:30 a.m.

AS FAR AS SCHOOL DAYS go, the first day of school is usually a good day, everything being fresh and brand-new. The air is not yet stale with the distinct odor of teenagers, the hallways are glistening with a new coat of the vomit-colored paint that mysteriously decorates high schools all across America, and everyone carries just-purchased backpacks and binders that have yet to be covered in the doodling one is sure to do while bored in yet another pointless calculus class. A thick cloud of possibility hangs over the entire day until, by three p.m., you've found yourself sufficiently settled into the mundane groove of the whole thing and you can't believe you have to do this BS every day for another nine months.

My summer had been pretty dull, spent with my parents at a theater and dance festival in Vermont that my mom ran. You would think that a summer with a bunch of artists in the middle of the woods would be rather fun, but really it just ends up being a bunch of entitled people debating Thoreau and blowing smoke up each other's asses. I'd never been creative and doubted I ever would be. I'd spent the majority of my life yearning to be creative, or to be something, somebody. Despite having two parents who couldn't be more artistic and focused if they tried, I was born with zero creativity or spark or uniqueness. I'd never had such purpose. Even at a no-name camp in the woods, I was a nobody, plain and simple.

And I wasn't just creativity challenged. My grades sucked and always had. I'd never won an award or gotten an A. I'd never known what to say in a "What do you want to be when you grow up?" question scenario. I'd literally never caught a ball in my life, and when it came to making friends I was as popular as the wilted salads they sell at Starbucks. (I ask you, what kind of monster drinks coffee and eats arugula at the same time, anyway?)

In short, I had no idea who I was, I doubted I ever would, and if there had been an end-of-year high school award for the biggest pessimist, I would've won with flying colors.

I'd made it all the way to junior year with only one real friend. Audrey hated high school with the kind of hyped-up ferocity usually reserved for war or professional sporting events. It was as if she was politically opposed to the idea of education and teenagers in general, referring to our peers as *them* with a thick air of disdain and suspicion in her voice.

Despite her short and scrawny seventeen-year-old frame, Audrey maintained the regal demeanor of a middle-aged grande dame of the theater. Her accent had an antique ring to it, with words handpicked from black-and-white movies where women wore gloves to lunch and slapped people without repercussion.

"Why are they smiling? What is going on with these people?!" Audrey heaved, nervously clutching the strap of the 100 percent Italian leather hatbox she insisted on using in place of a backpack. "What do they know that we don't?"

Two giggly freshmen girls walked by us, squealing at the realization that they had homeroom together. Audrey winced like someone with a terrible hangover at a monster truck rally.

"I've said it before and I'll say it again, Audrey. The harsh reality is that some of these people *enjoy* this," I said, examining the mobs darting to and from their lockers. It would've been impossible for me to hate school as much as Audrey did, but I was definitely a close second. The one thing Audrey had over me was that she had a dream, which is the first step to a purpose. Whereas I didn't want to be anything, Audrey wanted to be an actress. She was very into our school drama club—and I mean *very*. She lived life like a three-act play, yet it was never clear which act she was in. She was dead set on becoming a world-renowned star.

The only problem was that she wasn't very good.

In fact, she was genuinely terrible onstage.

Still, talent and ability aside, the stage provided Audrey with the vehicle with which to find the version of herself she wanted to be. It didn't matter that she wasn't the best; she loved it too much to care.

"Why do I get the feeling this is going to be a particularly long year?" Audrey said as she spun the lock on her locker, then dumped a few textbooks inside with an echoed thud.

Just as I began to agree, a mound of very curly blond hair appeared in the crowd. As people passed and the crowd cleared, I was struck by this face, this weirdly adorable face. It was like no other face I'd seen before. Sparkly eyes, one greener than the other. A slightly crooked nose. Freckled cheeks. Lips that looked drawn on. A jawline that could've gotten a job cutting stained-glass windows. The kind of perfectly broad shoulders you can only be born with, in the kind of fitted T-shirt you can only get away with if you were born that way.

As of that particular moment I had never even kissed a boy, so my being gay was as theoretical as it was irrevocable. My gaydar had never been all that dependable. Regardless, something about this kid was alerting my internal radar of a deep, proximate homosexuality. This, of course, could have been another glitch in the system of desperation. But I was instantaneously hoping it wasn't.

Needless to say, I was staring.

"Hello? Marley? Hello?" Audrey was tapping my shoulder, bringing me back to earth. "What just happened? Are you having a stroke? If you die and I have to go through this entire school year without you, I will dig up your body and kill you all over again, so help me God."

"Sorry. What?" I asked, like someone attempting to have a conversation while constructing a model airplane in under three minutes.

"That kid's dad is famous." Audrey watched the curly-haired boy as he stopped, staring down at his map of the school like a tourist lost in Times Square.

"Which boy?" I asked, my voice cracking in a way it hadn't since the early stages of puberty.

"The one you're staring at like he's bacon." She sneered as she slammed her locker, the loud clang jolting me out of my stupor. "His dad is that preacher on TV. The one with those infomercials that air in the middle of the night where he and his wife shout scripture at you and sell DVDs. Can you believe they still have infomercials?"

"Forget infomercials. I can't believe they still sell DVDs."

"Come on, you've seen Reverend Jim. He's everywhere. He's like Dr. Phil, but instead of screaming at people to lose weight and deal with their daddy issues, he tells them to buy his products so they can get into heaven."

Like pretty much everyone else in America, I had seen Reverend Jim on TV. He was usually on one of those talking head "news" shows, blaming hurricanes on gay people or terrorist attacks on transgender people who used the "wrong" bathrooms. Reverend Jim was the antithesis of the world as I saw it and it panged me to discover that this insanely cute new kid was his spawn.

"Whatever you're thinking, ignore it," Audrey growled.

But I was already looking back down the hall, to see if I could spot him one more time. But it was too late—he was gone. He had long since disappeared into the sea of basic bitches that is high school. Isn't that the way the world always works? Things are never as good as they first seem. You see someone special, someone you find super cute, you get excited, then you realize they're the son of one of the country's most cele-brated bigots.

Or something like that.

"You know, Audrey." I sighed, zipping up my backpack. "I'm afraid you might be right about this being a long year."

But I had no idea.

No idea at all.

# NORTH CAROLINA TIMES

AUGUST 1

Famed televangelist Reverend Jim Anderson is relocating his religious empire from Branson, Missouri, to here in North Carolina. According to a spokesperson for the Ministry of the Good Word, the move is due to the substantially higher tax incentives offered to film crews in North Carolina. His wife, Angela, was born and raised in Winston-Salem, so the move is, according to the spokesperson, "a homecoming of sorts."

Reverend Jim has been a television staple for many years, known for his syndicated infomercials, on which he sells his numerous books and DVDs. Over the years, he has made headlines for opposing abortion rights and gay marriage, as well as being a strong defender of the controversial "pray-the-gay-away" movement and a proponent of prayer in schools.

Reverend Jim's followers are so numerous that over the past ten years he's estimated to have grossed over thirty million dollars from the sale of his products and speaking engagements. He is known online as the "Super Preacher," where he maintains a very popular blog among the fundamentalist Christian community.

He'll be making his first North Carolina speaking engagement this Sunday at the Greensboro Convention Center. Tickets are available on his website.

# MONDAY, SEPTEMBER 3,
## 1:45 p.m.

WHOEVER HAD THE IDEA TO schedule biology lab right after lunch must have had a really disgusting sense of humor. The mere words *biology* and *lab* make my stomach turn. Then add to it the reality that this is a class where one is expected to dissect actual frogs and owl pellets (aka owl poop), and you've got yourself a full-blown hour of comically extreme nausea. Especially when you've just eaten the food in our school's cafeteria, a level of gross so high it should've counted as its own science credit.

The teacher, Mrs. Spitz, a bony, long-haired old woman with such an eerie resemblance to a mop you would've thought she had been left there by the school janitor, was writing her name on the board.

"That's Spitz. Like what you do when extracting saliva," she explained with the enthusiasm of someone who would rather lick a car battery than have to do what she was doing. "Please open your textbooks to page one."

The entire class let out a mild groan, accompanied by the thud of textbooks hitting desks. I was just beginning to count the number of weeks until Christmas break when the door flew open and the entire contents of a backpack came spilling across the floor. Right after, I spied that same mound of curly blond hair from the morning crawling across the linoleum, apologizing with every step.

"Sorry!" he whispered in that way people whisper that isn't actually a whisper at all. "Keep going. I got lost on the other end of the school."

Mrs. Spitz rolled her eyes and let out a pathetic sigh. She continued going through the motions of her introduction, while the rest of the class continued going through the motions of pretending to listen. (Sometimes high school seemed a lot like the theater Audrey so dearly loved, each of us pretending to listen to the other for the sake of a story we were all stuck living in.)

"Okay. Page eight. 'Is yeast alive and does it live inside me?'" Mrs. Spitz read aloud.

The televangelist spawn plopped down in a spare seat in the second row. Despite my creepy staring, he didn't glance over, look up, or do anything close to noticing me at all.

Clearly, I was hideous, or my gaydar really needed to be replaced.

But I couldn't stop stealing glances at him. It was like my mind was stuck in the present but my eyes were hell-bent on the future.

# MONDAY, SEPTEMBER 3, 7:15 p.m.

THE PUNGENT SMELL OF BOILING kale and tofu had overtaken the kitchen, where my mom was preparing dinner from a cookbook called *The Psycho-Spiritual Diet and Lifestyle.*

"But that's the thing about lyrical dance, Marley—if we can't debate it, then why does it exist at all?" she asked, not pausing for me to answer before launching into an exhausting lecture on the importance of freethinking and pirouettes. After a solid ten minutes, she finally paused, tossing a pinch of Himalayan pink salt crystals and rosemary grown in our backyard into the kale, then asked me about my first day of school.

I shrugged. "It was fine."

"Marley, you know how Sharon and I feel about empty words like *fine*," my father said, appearing in the doorway and scratching his long gray beard like a cartoon version of the novelist he actually was. My parents had strict disdain for words like *fine* or *nice* or *okay*. They also asked to be addressed by their first names.

In a nutshell, they were nuts.

"In that case, my day was *overwhelming in its uneventful*

*demeanor.* Better?" I replied, to their delight. My parents could be a bit much when it came to their freethinking "intellectual" routine, but they meant well and loved me almost as much as they loved a well-rounded vocabulary.

"Your problem, Marley, is that you don't have a force that drives you," my mother said, launching into yet another dissection of my outlook on life. This was a common pastime of both my parents. "Sculpture, mixed media, advanced Pilates, anything. Every day, you need something to contribute to the world and be excited to wake up for."

I didn't have the heart or energy to explain to my mother that neither sculpture nor mixed media were high school activities (nor Pilates, for that matter), but I understood her point all too well. For my entire life I'd been the kid in class with no label. There was the football jock, the pretty cheerleader, the science weirdo, the cross-country star, the funny one, the bully, the smelly girl, the smelly boy, the band geek, the drama geek, the general all-around geek, and so on. In order to solidify your place in the community that is any form of school, you needed a label, and despite my best efforts, I'd never found one. Sure, there was the gay thing, but at this point being gay was like being a Pisces. By which I mean: common, and oftentimes emotionally unstable.

*Why can't sarcasm and global resentment be a passion?* I asked myself inside my head.

I cut the conversation with my parents short and beelined for my bedroom . . . where I immediately googled *Reverend Jim son.* I don't know what I was hoping to discover about this kid

I had so quickly become obsessed with. It took a while before Google served any help, since the first few hundred results were from bloggers in rebel flag T-shirts celebrating *Reverend Jim* as the *son* of God.

Finally, I found a biography of Reverend Jim's family, complete with a heavily staged family portrait in front of an enormous cross that had been painted red, white, and blue. Reverend Jim had a botoxed and chemically orange-colored face with a toupee so big it could've been considered its own species. His wife, Angela, had the biggest and fakest smile to ever be seen on a human being outside of paid amusement park performers.

Their only son, however, appeared normal.

And he had a name.

Christopher.

Even though he was stuck in a photo with the words *Jesus Junkies* written in calligraphy above his head, he looked just as cute as he had at school that morning. Unlike his parents', his smile seemed genuine and kind.

I clicked on a clip of Reverend Jim speaking to thousands of rabid fans at one of his many conventions. In between plugging his countless books and DVDs, he tore into America's "road to ruin paved in sin." The camera panned around to the audience of devotees frothing at every judgmental word.

The entire time Christopher sat onstage with his mother, behind his dad. He didn't respond to any of the theatrics, even though his mom kept jumping out of her chair and waving her arms around like she was afraid the air was attacking her.

I paused the clip at a moment where Christopher was close up in the frame, and stared into his eyes. He was a bit younger in the clip but he looked pretty much the same. I didn't know what I was hoping to find, but I was definitely searching for something, as if staring hard enough would tell me whether or not he liked boys. Or, more accurately, if it was possible that I could convince him to like *me*. I don't know what it was, but I could tell he wasn't like his parents. And not just because I thought he was cute . . . although maybe that played a large part of it. But, regardless, I could feel it in my gut.

He was different. And I was determined to find out how.

# TUESDAY, SEPTEMBER 4, 8:00 a.m.

I RUSHED TO MY LOCKER the minute I got to school, making it the first time I'd ever rushed to do *anything* at school. I would not have admitted it in the moment, but I didn't want to miss the opportunity to see Reverend Jim's son again. Audrey was snaking her way through the crowd, wearing an unseasonably heavy coat, sunglasses, and clutching one of those enormous Starbucks cups that's so big it might as well be a novelty bucket.

"Are we even allowed to bring lattes to school, Audrey?" I asked as she sucked the caramel-colored coffee through the green straw like some fabulous recovering alcoholic fashion designer making her post-rehab debut.

"Do I look like I care?" she said, her eyes rolling in a perfect circular motion. "Plus, it's a flat white."

The truth was, she looked like someone who didn't care about anything, or rather, someone who worked really hard to look like she didn't care about anything. I nodded, distracted, as I stared through the crowd.

"What am I missing?" she asked, attempting to join my gaze. I snapped back to reality long enough to start saying "Nothing," when he appeared, a few feet away within the crowd. I froze, staring at him like an awestruck pioneer discovering the Grand Canyon. He was wearing a red hoodie that you could tell was brand-new, in that way brand-new clothes always look like costumes on a TV show. His hair was messy but in that way where you can tell someone used just the right products to make it look messy. He had this natural lightness, a glow or something, that seemed to radiate off the lockers and linoleum floors. In short, my feelings were so obvious and on the nose that even I resented me.

He passed, without a word. He smiled, but not the kind of smile that would've been too much for eight a.m. A light, warm, totally not obnoxious smile. And not a fake one like the ones his parents seemed to make in every photo I'd found in my all-night Google black hole of all things Reverend Jim and company. Then he was gone. It was quiet for a moment before Audrey tapped me on the shoulder.

"Hello? You in there, darling?" she called right into my eardrum.

"Sorry. Yes." I could feel myself floating back down from the clouds.

"You can't possibly be crushing over the son of the biggest and most conservative preacher superstar in the world, can you?" Audrey asked.

"Audrey, I don't know what's going on with me. I don't even know this guy—there's just something about him that I can't stop thinking about. I feel like he's different from his family. Listen to me! I sound ridiculous."

"You definitely do, darling." Audrey nodded. "Who kidnapped Marley and replaced him with his optimistic evil twin? I don't like this plot twist! If you start getting giddy, what the hell are we going to bond over?"

I'd made snarky my main defining feature, observing the world so sarcastically you would've thought I was a professional blogger. Audrey and I had *always* shared an overall mood of being over it. It had started when we were on the same team in fifth-grade dodgeball and I'd overheard Audrey mutter "Please just kill me" to herself—I knew instantaneously that we'd be fast friends.

"Whatever is happening," she continued, placing her ring-clad fingers on my shoulder in a rare moment of warmth, the kind of moment she wouldn't be able to pull off onstage, "it's *extremely* entertaining to watch. So, when are you going to, oh, I don't know, talk to him?"

I felt my face turn the color of his hoodie. Before I could find an answer, the homeroom bell rang.

# TUESDAY, SEPTEMBER 4,
# 7:45 p.m.

MY MOM HAD A HABIT of forgetting something literally every time she went to the supermarket. She was never one for lists, choosing instead to "live in the moment of the shopping experience." Which is all well and good, until you forget tampons and decide it's a cool idea to send your seventeen-year-old son to pick them up for you after dinner.

"Make sure you get the heavy flow kind!" she screamed at me from the front door as I drove away from the house.

Once I got to the supermarket, I made my way over to the appropriate section, the aisle composed solely of tampons and adult diapers. The aisle that all but screams, "The human body is very messy!" Luckily, the coast was clear, not a soul in sight. I hastily examined all the options, searching for the words *heavy flow*, and eventually found what I was looking for. Just as I was reaching for the twelve-pack, a voice spoke up behind me.

"Can I help you find anything?"

It startled me so much that I dropped the pack of feminine hygiene products on the floor. "They're for my mom," I said loudly, turning around as if I had been caught shoplifting.

That's when my jaw dropped and the world came to a screeching halt.

Shut the front door, it was him!

Curly hair, freckles, jawline, crooked nose, two-toned eyeballs, that smile, everything!

"Um. Okay," Christopher said, stifling a hopefully non-patronizing laugh. "Don't we go to school together?"

I was having a hard time forming the appropriate response; something as simple as "Yes, hi, I'm Marley" would have sufficed. But words weren't forming, so after what felt like a five-hour-long awkward pause, I nodded.

"I'm Christopher."

"Marley. I've seen you before," I said flatly, sounding much more like a serial killer than I'd intended. "I mean, at school. Are you new?"

"Sure am. Just moved here from Branson, Missouri. Ever been?"

I shook my head to express my no, since I'd taken further use of words off the table for the time being.

"It's basically Las Vegas for conservative Christians and the people who love them. So none of the casinos and hookers . . . but triple the buffets!" He grinned like someone up to something.

Just what he was up to was yet to be determined.

He beamed confidence and a surprising element of smoothness you usually don't see from people outside the hip-hop community. I was like, *What could you possibly have done to ooze such coolness?*

It isn't every day that you find yourself having a crush on a celebrity preacher's son. And it's even rarer that you find yourself talking to him while standing over a fallen box of tampons. So needless to say, I was having a very hard time reading the situation. His charming grin could mean one of two things: Either he was bragging about coming from said Las Vegas for conservative Christians, or he too was registering it as one of the most hilariously nightmarish places in the history of mankind. I was in no condition to tell the difference, so I changed the subject.

"And you work here?" I asked, which was a dumb question unless I thought he was wearing a name tag for fun.

"I do. I worked at a supermarket in Branson, so when we moved my parents made me get a job at the one here. My parents are obsessed with two things: responsibility and Jesus. But you might have already figured that?"

I didn't know whether to pretend I hadn't already figured out who his family was or to admit I knew he was one of the Andersons. If I did, that might indicate that I had stalked him. Which, clearly, I had. But I didn't want to come across as creepy on the off chance that my oft-malfunctioning gaydar had been right.

"Uh-huh," I mumbled, blushing like a closeted gay teenager seeing *Magic Mike XXL* with his parents on summer break. (Not that I speak from experience.) My flustered skin made him giggle. Even his giggle was cool, calm, and collected.

"So, you're gay, right?" he asked, flat out, like he was asking if I'd ever tried water.

This, obviously, caught me so off guard that I forgot my own name, birth date, and phone number. His confident grin awaited my answer. Was he gearing up to save me? Was he going to baptize me with the mouthwash an aisle over? He was so cute that, quite frankly, I wondered if I was going to let him.

His cool, calm collectedness fell into momentary confusion. "Sorry. Was that too forward? I can be blunt. I was just curious because you've been blushing and your voice has gone up, like, five octaves in the few minutes we've been talking to each other. Also you are, like, *flaming*."

I must have looked like I was going to faint because he quickly laughed reassuringly.

"I'm kidding! I'm just messing with you." He slapped me on the shoulder, so hard that I almost went back to assuming he was straight. "I only asked if you're gay because I'm gay and I'm new here and, well, I don't have any friends. And you *have* been staring at me at school."

There are those moments in life where you literally pinch yourself to make sure you aren't dreaming and you feel ridiculous for pinching yourself because it's clichéd. Also you usually pinch too hard and it kind of hurts. This was one of those moments. I had absolutely no idea what was happening, but in retrospect I guess it's safe to say this was the moment where Christopher and I began.

"I *AM* GAY!" I said, eagerly and loudly, like I was coming out before Congress or the Thanksgiving dinner table. I was getting this entire situation so wrong that a more self-aware part of me wanted to laugh. "Sorry. I am *not* handling this well, am I?"

"I mean . . ."

Christopher winked, leaning down to pick up the package of tampons sitting on the tile floor between us. He handed them to me with a grin I could only imagine Reverend Jim would've deemed sinful.

"Let's start over," he said. Then he took my hand and shook it, with a firm, gentlemanly grip. "I'll see you at school tomorrow."

I shook back. "I believe that is absolutely true."

He smiled. "Good." Our hands went back to being hands, and not a frankly romantic bridge between us. "Now, I'm afraid there are some soup cans in aisle eight that need my attention."

"And I better get these to my mom before . . . oh God . . . never mind."

Smiling, he walked away, head held high, like he did this all the time. Like stealing hearts was just another hobby. Like he was some sort of retail Casanova. Like his father wasn't a famously antigay TV preacher and like we weren't in the middle of a grocery store on a weeknight in North Carolina. Something special had just occurred, I could feel it, the way dogs can sense storms. I watched him go, in utter awe of the entire encounter, then paid for the tampons and took them home to my mom.

And that, my friends, is what I call romance.

# NOW

IT'S WEIRD TO THINK BACK on those first few days of seeing Christopher. How it felt as if with each moment I was
around him, he chipped away at my snarky armor just a little
bit more. How unattainable he seemed. How high a pedestal I
put him on. I guess that's something a lot of us do when we
meet people we like: We make them into these supreme beings.
Everything they do seems like it's the first time in history anyone has ever done it—because the only history that really
matters is your own history. People's faces change, from the
time you meet them to when you actually get to know them. I
don't know if it's that their image settles into your brain, making it less foreign, less brand-new or whatever. It's like when
you go somewhere you've never been before, like when we first
went to Vermont. You see everything for the first time, you get
lost, you wonder what's inside certain buildings, down certain
roads, what certain signs mean. Then, by the end of your trip,
everything seems normal, everything seems everyday, like it's
yours. Not in a bad way either, just comfortingly familiar, and
when you think back on what seemed so mysterious about it

all, you can't remember what it was because now it's just a part of you.

That's what getting to know someone feels like. One day you see them; they intrigue you; you have so many questions and you wonder if you'll ever have a chance to ask them all. Then, a few weeks in, you know them so well you can't imagine a day without them. You know the indention in their chest, the birth-mark on their armpit, the way they absolutely detest jalapeños. They have become a part of your routine. Or at least that's how it felt with Christopher.

It happened absurdly fast, our falling for each other. But sometimes things click—and also, it's not like two gay teenagers in some small North Carolina town have that much else going on. By the end of those few weeks, I felt like I could've drawn his face from memory, every freckle and crease (and I am truly terrible at drawing). I couldn't imagine a night without texting him good night. I couldn't imagine a morning without kiss-ing him by my locker. I couldn't imagine him being a stranger ever again.

Even now, when I see his picture—when they show it in one of my interviews, or when I stumble upon it on Instagram—it feels like he's still here. Like nothing ever happened. Like our routines are still routine. Like, when I get under the covers, he'll text me good night with some stupid emoji that I hate. (Christopher loved emojis, but hey—we all have our faults.)

When you get to know someone so well that they're ingrained in your memory forever, it'll always feel like you could reach out and touch them. Even after all the twisting and spinning of our stories, even after he's gone, he still remains, safely inside my mind. As if he never left at all.

# WEDNESDAY, SEPTEMBER 5, 11:45 p.m.

I COULDN'T SLEEP. I WAS doing that thing where you are trying so desperately to pass out that you cover your face in pillows and blankets in hope that the darkness will trick your body into thinking it's already asleep and then your mind will follow through. (This has never worked for me or anyone else in the history of insomnia . . . but regardless, we continue to try.)

The reality was that this wasn't insomnia but mere excitement, a feeling somewhat foreign to my aggressively boring life. Christopher had stirred something in me—and no, I don't mean in my pants, though, okay, maybe down there too. Something about the sparkle in his eyes made the world feel a little less black and white. Something about the way he looked at me made the voices in my head that had always told me that my life would never stray from the ordinary get quieter and quieter.

I got up to get a glass of water. Why do we always do that when we can't sleep? As if making yourself need to pee will do anything close to good. Regardless, I was filling a glass from the elaborate filtered pitcher my mother's guru had given her for her birthday when I noticed a light on in my dad's office.

Dad never stayed up later than ten . . . and even then it was a rarity. So I knew something was going on.

I tapped the partially open office door.

There was a moment of startled rustling, followed by Dad's distracted voice.

"Hello?"

I poked my head in. Dad's usually organized desk was covered in papers.

"Everything okay?" I asked. Dad's face fell to a panicked expression.

"Yes. Of course. I'm just doing some work. Why? Do you think something is wrong?" he rambled in the way you do when something is clearly and most definitely wrong.

"Just checking."

Everywhere you looked in Dad's office there was something interesting to catch your eye, whether it was a mask from some tribe he and my mother visited in New Zealand or a Mongolian tea set gifted to him by the witch doctor who'd come and stayed with us last Christmas break.

"What're you doing up?" Dad asked, taking a drink from a glass filled with a brown liquid that was clearly not his usual evening kombucha.

"I couldn't sleep. Are you . . . drinking?"

Flustered, he set the glass down on a coaster carved out of petrified wood he'd picked up in Bosnia. He removed his glasses and massaged his temples.

"Please don't tell Sharon."

I had seen my father drink on two prior occasions: once at my aunt Gail's wedding, which was such a debacle that the invitation should've come with a two-drink minimum, and once the night my grandfather died. Needless to say, seeing my father with a drink was not a sign of good news.

"What's going on?" I asked, letting myself into the room and closing the door behind me. Dad cleared his throat and motioned for me to have a seat.

"I screwed up, Marley."

"How so?"

His eyes scanned the countless papers spread across his desk as if the papers were poisonous snakes waiting to attack. He stared down at them intensely.

"I think we're losing the house."

He said this casually, so matter-of-fact it almost seemed like he was telling me what we'd be having for dinner in two weeks' time.

"We're *what*?"

He stood up and paced over to his bookshelf. I looked closer at the papers and realized they were bills.

"You might not remember this, but about ten years ago your mother decided to let me be in charge of the bookkeeping around here. She'd done it herself for so long and she hated it. Then, once she got promoted to head of her department at school, she basically said, 'What am I trying to prove?' and turned everything over to me."

Mom had always been the alpha in our family—a sweet,

gentle alpha, but the alpha for sure. Before Mom, Dad had been your average Joe, but after a few months together she had turned him into the hippie he had been ever since. She called all the shots, so for her to allow Dad to take the reins of something was probably the hardest thing she'd done since choreographing that three-hour ballet to the soundtrack of *Die Hard 2*.

"So, fine," I said. "You do the bookkeeping. What happened?" My eyes zoomed in on the words PAST DUE and FINAL NOTICE printed across so many of the bills in front of him.

"Well, my last book wasn't the hit we all thought it would be," he said, tapping the bookshelf full of extra copies of *Boston Tea Party Zombie Apocalypse*. "The publisher put a lot behind it and I stupidly took on some loans in anticipation of all the royalties that would come rolling in. How was I to know that another author and another publisher would put out *Boston Tea Party Zombie Massacre* two months before my book came out? Anyway, the bank doesn't like excuses—they just like to be paid back. Which I haven't been able to do. And, to make matters worse, instead of telling your mother, I took out *another* line of credit against the house because I really believed we'd be fine. I thought I'd get another deal as big as the last one and pay everything off in one big chunk. That's how it had happened in the past, so I was sure everything would work itself out."

The words fell out of his mouth quickly, as if spending too much time with them inside his mouth might make him sick. He took the last swig of his drink and put the glass down atop one of the many bills, creating a wet ring over the words FINAL NOTICE.

"Dad—"

He cut me off, sitting back down at his desk.

"Greg. Please."

"Fine. Greg. You have to tell Mom. You can't keep this a secret. You can't lie to her and pretend everything is fine when clearly it's not."

Unable to stay in one place, he stood up from his desk again. "I know. I know. I thought I'd fix this first; I thought I'd make it work and then it'd be fine and she'd never have to know. But . . . well, it's not. And now I don't know how to tell her or when to tell her. And I can't do it now—she's got so much on her plate at work. Also, you know how she gets when Mercury is in retrograde."

I decided to ignore the issue of retrograde; I was not in the mood to debate astrology with my moderately tipsy and extremely panicked father in the middle of the night.

"But . . ." I started without really knowing what to follow up with. I just knew that the conversation couldn't end yet. We had to figure something out.

"I don't know, Marley. Maybe what's most important isn't the truth but making sure everyone gets through whatever is going on and can come out on the other side for the better."

"And lying to Mom is going to make things better?"

He sat down on the bench beside me. "It isn't a lie if the intention is right, Marley. I just need more time to try and fix this."

He stared at me, eye to eye. His were reddish and puffy. It

was strange to see them without his glasses. His face looked entirely different.

"Do you really believe that, Dad?"

He was quiet for a while. I could hear the creaks of our old house, the only house I'd ever lived in, the one my father might have lost.

"I want to. I really, really want to."

# THURSDAY, SEPTEMBER 6, 10:31 a.m.

AUDREY TEXTED ME DURING CLASS to A) remind me, yet again, how much she hated school and B) say we should go to the showing of *Charade* at our independent movie theater the following night. We were in agreement on both topics. We had a rule: I watched old movies with her if she watched garbage reality television with me. It was the best of both worlds.

Between the kismet-like run-in with Christopher at the supermarket, the late-night confession from my father, and the fact that Christopher had said hi to me three times already and it wasn't even lunch, it was turning out to be a pretty memorable week. And the last time I'd had a memorable week was the week I'd been home with a stomach flu and Bravo had aired a marathon of the entire *Real Housewives of Beverly Hills* series from start to finish.

I was moderately out of it—and not just because I was listening to the coma-inducing voice of our history teacher, Mr. Bannockburn. (Honestly, though, if you're going to try and teach a group of teenagers about the Cold War, drink a Red

Bull first.) I hadn't really been able to sleep after the encounter with my father. I had never seen him so stressed out. The threat of losing the house my parents had always referred to as their "temple of family" was no joke. It's a disturbing feeling the day you realize your parents are just as screwed up as you are. I was lost in thought, weighing whether or not to say something to Mom before it was too late, when the bell rang and it was time for lunch.

In a daze I wandered over to the cafeteria. Eleven fifteen is an obnoxiously early time to serve vegetable lasagna, but that didn't stop the cafeteria ladies from doing it. I was halfway through the very long line when I happened to look up through my bangs and spot Christopher a few people ahead of me. With his brand-new backpack and all-American plaid button-up, he looked like an advertisement for the perfect teenager. He glanced up from his phone just as my staring had crossed the line from *noticing someone you know* to *creepy weirdo who probably drives a windowless van*. He smiled, only intensifying the all-American motif.

"There you are!" he shouted over the hubbub of the cafeteria. "Come over!"

He grinned at me so knowingly that I wondered if he knew who he was talking to. He kept motioning to me while I stood where I was, halfway smiling. Carefully, I made my way over, hoping I hadn't made the mistake of thinking he was talking to me when in fact he had been talking to some gorgeous baseball player behind me the whole time.

"Sorry . . . were you talking to me?" I asked. Then I added, a little too loudly, "Oh! Were you trying to help me cut in line ahead of all these other people?"

The few people paying attention heard me and gave us the kind of angry faces you give to people who blatantly ignore the rules. Christopher let me into the line beside him, lying loud enough for people around to hear.

"Don't be silly; I was saving your spot in line while you were in the bathroom."

He squeezed my arm—a squeeze that sent a shiver down my spine and made me a little dizzy for a second or two. Then he whispered for me to go with it. This was the first time in history a cute boy had whispered something in my ear. This was the first time in history a cute boy had done anything whatsoever to my ear. We exchanged mischievous smiles, and I delighted in having something to share with him.

We got to the front, the lunch ladies flopping the slices of room-temperature pasta onto our trays without so much as a smile or the apology each of us so rightfully deserved. We found a table close enough to the salad bar and band geeks that no one was sitting at it.

"Sorry. I can be a little slow when it comes to stuff like that," I said sheepishly, flinging my backpack onto the chair. This was a lie; I was almost *never* slow when it came to screwing over my peers.

"Slow at what? Deception?" he asked, so straight-faced I was taken aback. It must have shown on my face because he immediately smiled and told me, "Kidding. Obviously."

Being behind on the joke was new to me, seeing as Audrey

and I had our own language when it came to quipping about our rotten lives. Yet something about Christopher slowed me down or threw me off track from my usual avenue of sarcasm and highway of general snark. Up until he first smiled at me, I had lived my life so comfortably sarcastic and quippy that Audrey had always said I'd be a natural celebrity on Twitter. I would have joined Twitter by this point if it were still relevant or if I had the ambition—and that's when you know you're in trouble, when you're too lazy to tweet.

"Is it just me or is eleven fifteen an offensive time to serve vegetable lasagna?" he asked before stuffing a bite of the afore-mentioned entrée into his mouth. I felt a tingle in my heart.

"Someone should be arrested," I added, staring at mine like it was a sculpture in a modern art museum. This made Christopher burst out laughing, which made me feel like the million dollars someone would pay for the sculpture in said modern art museum.


And we were off. Joke, joke, zing, zing. We effortlessly recapped the first half of our days to each other, like we did this all the time. We built upon each other's punch lines, interrupted each other's stories, finished each other's sentences. He was genuinely making me laugh, and not in the way you pretend to laugh at everything a cute boy says at a party when you're hoping he'll have too many beers and forget he's straight. It was all happening so organically, the way it always seems to in angsty teen movies in which attractive heterosexual white kids accomplish stuff.

Despite his humor, he had a positive outlook on the whole school thing, pointing out that we were stuck there whether we bitched about it or not, so why waste the breath bitching? It was odd to be around someone with such a naturally happy attitude. It's not that Audrey and I were *total* haters . . . but it would be a lie to say that complaining wasn't one of our main hobbies. I wasn't used to trying to see the good in something like school or, well, anything, but Christopher seemed to do so without any effort whatsoever. The Internet teaches people to judge things, not see things . . . and I was very much a child of the Internet.

He swung back and forth between funny and sarcastic, sweet and surprising. He was the best of both worlds and above taking anything too seriously. He seemed unfazed by so many of the trivial things that would send me or Audrey into a total bitchfest. Like, how loud the band geeks were being as they discussed the latest developments in some computer game made specifically for band geeks and single, middle-aged men. Yet despite his positivity, he wasn't one of those obnoxious people who was *always* happy. There was still the right amount of unspecified pain in his eyes for me to identify with him on a human level. This was an immense relief, because next to people who raise monkeys as their children, nothing is creepier to me than being 100 percent happy all the time.

"How long have you been here?" he asked, looking around the cafeteria. I couldn't help but imagine us as prisoners, me as the old-timer and him as the newbie fresh off his arrest for something a reader could sympathize with, like robbing an Apple Store after hours.

"Too long. But since middle school, to be exact," I explained. "What was your last school like?"

He started to answer but had a mouth full of food, so instead he nodded until he'd finished chewing. I had never seen someone look so cute chewing with marinara sauce all over their chin—and Audrey had forced me to sit through every *Godfather* movie. Twice.

"It was a private school, actually. Super-duper conservative and stuffy. It's where all the big Branson preachers send their kids."

"Yikes." I winced, thinking that my school sucked, but at least I didn't have conservative nut jobs judging my every move. Aside from the handful of typical school bullies, the only person who'd had a hard time accepting me was myself . . . but that guy was a total jerk anyway.

"It wasn't so bad. It was a good school—there were a couple of mean teachers, but otherwise people were always really nice," he said, before adding, "but that might just be because my dad's famous."

"What about when you came out?" I asked carefully, feeling a bit too much like a reporter pretending to be sympathetic on a morning news program.

"Most kids at school were fine. Same with the teachers. My parents were a different story."

"How so?"

"Come on, Marley—my dad is literally Reverend Jim

Anderson. You can imagine the shit storm that occurred when his only son was revealed to be the absolute worst thing he thinks a person can be."

"Did they kick you out or something?"

"Oh God, no! That would be *un-Christian* of them." He rolled his eyes. "No, instead they did the right thing . . . and tried to brainwash me. Have you ever heard of pray-the-gay-away camps?"

"Holy crap! You went to one of those places?!" I gasped. I'd heard about that kind of stuff on the news, but never in a million years came close to experiencing anything like it myself.

He nodded, wiping the marinara off his chin. "Yeah. It was pretty weird, but I didn't take it seriously, and eventually they basically just gave up on me and let me go read in my cabin for the rest of the summer. I spent most of the camp finally reading *The Hunger Games*—which was fitting because we were stuck in the woods and pretty much everyone there wanted to kill me," he deadpanned, then added after an awkward pause, "Kidding. I mean, about people wanting to kill me, not the reading *The Hunger Games* part. Speaking of which, doesn't the dystopian future sound terrible?!"

I couldn't believe he could be so casual about all of this. I knew if what he was talking about had happened to me, I wouldn't have been able to get over it. I would be scarred for life. I'm really good at pretending that I'm rubber and that all problems in life bounce off of me, but the reality is I'm closer to glue. Things stick to me; I've just gotten really good at pretending they're not there.

"But what about when you got home?" I asked. "Were your parents upset that it didn't work or whatever?"

He thought about this for a moment, then shrugged. "Yeah, but I basically said to them, 'If you don't bug me about it, I won't bug you about it. Or we can make it a huge thing and I'll run away and we'll never speak to each other again and you'll have to explain to all your followers why your son has disappeared.' You've seen my dad and all his crazy disciples on TV, right?"

Having listened to his father's speeches online, I wanted to reach out, squeeze him, bring him home to my mom and dad, and show him what real acceptance was like. But mainly I just wanted to squeeze him. He looked very squeezable.

"Yeah. I googled him," I admitted.

"Pretty intense, huh?" He laughed tragically. "But that was the real clincher for them, the realization that it'd be easier to have a gay kid who didn't talk about being gay than it would be to explain to the public why their son ran away."

"Are they really that terrible?" I asked, maybe a little too forwardly, but it was too late to take it back.

"They're not terrible. I know it sounds like they are. Believe me, they've said some terrible things to me, but they mean well. They're just incredibly screwed up." His empathy was making him increasingly attractive, but that also might have been the way the sunlight was bouncing off the spit guard surrounding the salad bar and hitting his natural highlights.

"But don't you want to shake them and make them understand? Make them get that what they believe is wrong? All the crap your dad spews is so—" I cut myself off because I could feel myself getting too fired up.

"Yes. Of course I hate the crap he spews. And of course I want to shake them and make them understand. But isn't that what they've done to me? How would me doing it to them be any better? Spew is spew, no matter who is saying it."

"Because you're actually right and they're not."

He shrugged again and took a sip of his chocolate milk. A disgusting thing to drink with Italian food of any kind, but he looked so adorable doing it that I let it pass.

"I just can't believe how okay you are after something like that. Or at least you seem to be," I said, weighing how offensive the words might sound as I spoke them. "Is that a weird thing to say?"

"No. It's not. And I appreciate that. No one's ever told me that before." He smiled at me, the same sweet smile from the grocery store and from the hallway the other day. It was quiet between us, just the murmur of the cafeteria. I wanted to kiss him, but that would've, at the very least, required we venture into an alternate universe where I had confidence, and I'd left my passport at home.

I had so many more things I wanted to learn about him. I didn't want our conversation to end. I wanted to know every single detail about him. I wanted to sit at this lunch table for the rest of the day, or week, or year, or lifetime, and just learn about him and only him.

I magically summoned the nerve to take his hand.

"I'm sorry you've been through crap like that," I told him, my eyes awkwardly darting up at the ceiling and all around the room at everything but his own sparkling set.

He nodded a thank-you and took an enormous bite of the pasta. Then he said, "Okay, so this might sound totally lame, and if so feel free to say no, but I have to go to my aunt's fiftieth birthday party tomorrow night. It's a barbecue and I'm fairly certain it will be completely boring but it'd fun to have someone with me to talk to and roll my eyes with. Plus, it'll totally piss off my parents to see me bring a date."

A date? His words unleashed a flurry of rainbow-colored butterflies in my stomach so hard that I thought they might come flying out of my mouth and descend upon the whole cafeteria. He was so strong and confident, and he wasn't one of those cheerful robots I'd feared he might be. He was someone with the crap of the world in his eyes, but unlike me, he could also see the beauty. I couldn't believe what was happening, but he was someone I could see myself really, really liking, and from the way he nervously grinned, awaiting my answer, I could tell he might really, really like me too.

"Definitely!" I said, as excitedly as a seventeen-year-old boy can sound when agreeing to go to some random woman's fiftieth birthday party.

It was a date.

An actual, genuine date.

# Friday, September 7, 3:32 p.m.

THE SCHOOL DAY HAD MOVED by at whatever is slower than a snail's pace, and I spent the majority of that time going back and forth between staring at the photos of Christopher sitting behind his dad at church that I'd found online and dreaming about how in Denmark I've heard people only have to go to school for three hours a day.

I had promised Audrey I'd come cheer her on at the callbacks for the fall musical, *Into the Woods*. So instead of tracking down Christopher, after school I sat in the back of the school auditorium, a cinder-block building that had been there since the seventies and resembled a prison far more than a home for entertainment of any kind. (That said, if you'd been there for the previous spring's production of *Hello, Dolly!* you most definitely would've considered it a form of capital punishment.)

Audrey was up next to sing—something she did with even less skill than her acting. I said a silent prayer as the school choir teacher plunked out the first few notes of Audrey's song.

As she began to belt in a key not documented on a music chart of any kind, I felt so proud to call her my best friend. She was effortless, grand, and oddly captivating in that way only super-drunk people on parade floats can be. There was no universe in which she could've possibly gotten the role she was auditioning for. All that aside, her peers and I clapped politely when she finished. I never would've told her how much I admired her tenacity because she would've undoubtedly never shut up about it.

We texted and arranged to meet outside the building, as there were only so many high school theater auditions I could watch without losing my mind.

I waited outside as the double doors burst open and Audrey came through them, out of breath and noticeably sweaty. She ripped off the pair of big white sunglasses she was wearing as she exited, an affectation that made zero sense since she was coming from inside to outside—but the grand gesture achieved whatever it was she was hoping for.

"Tell me the truth, darling! Was I divine or was I divine?" she brayed. (Somehow Audrey had the voice of a decade-long cigarette smoker even though she'd never touched a cigarette in her life.)

"You sure were something!" I said as convincingly as one could. I had learned a lot about "backstage behavior" after years of seeing Audrey as well as my mother's bizarre dance concerts. Rule of thumb: It is always better to nod and agree with the insane thing you've just witnessed than to actually respond truthfully. No one in entertainment of any kind wants to hear your honest opinion. Ever.

Audrey thanked me graciously, as if I had just presented her with a Lifetime Achievement Tony Award, before diving into a hyperactive rant of weekend plans.

"So we're on, right? For tonight, I mean. *Charade* at the Stevens Center? It's a new print and everything!"

Dammit. I had screwed up. I was so accustomed to having no one else to hang out with that I had totally forgotten about our plans when I had agreed to Christopher's party. And I had zero intention of bailing out on *that*.

"Crap," I said. Audrey's eyes immediately dissolved into the pissed-off glare she could give like no one else. "You know that guy, right? Christopher?" She nodded, the way you do when you're waiting for someone to get to the end of their story before you attack them with a salad fork. "He invited me to his aunt's birthday party and I really want to go. I know I shouldn't have agreed because I already made plans with you, but look, how often do I cancel on you?"

This question was the best I could come up with and was, admittedly, pretty weak. But it came from a real place.

"Let me get this straight. You're canceling on me outside of my drama club callbacks for the fall musical to go on a date with the gay kid you're obsessed with? Oh my God—my life is a rerun of *Glee*, isn't it?"

We both laughed, so I knew we were okay. I breathed a sigh of relief as she gripped my wrist and stared directly into my eyes.

"Just never do it again. Deal?"

"Deal," I said, terrified and faithful.

My wrist visibly bruised.

# FRIDAY, SEPTEMBER 7, 6:06 p.m.

I CHANGED OUTFITS MORE TIMES than I care to admit. It was like a scene out of a bad movie where your hapless leading man is getting ready for a first date where hilarious hijinks will ensue. The kind of movie where everything ends perfectly and there's an obnoxiously cute dog in it that gives a better performance than 90 percent of the cast. In short: I was a nervous, clichéd wreck preparing for not only my first date with Christopher but my first date ever.

I finally settled on a blue sweater I'd gotten last Christmas that still had the tags on it. I wasn't much for "dressing up," but maybe that was because I'd never had an occasion to do so. Or maybe I was just lazy.

My parents were listening to old records and dancing around the kitchen while they cooked some terrible-smelling meal involving eggplant and pickled seaweed. The fear that had filled my father's eyes two nights ago was nowhere to be found, and Mom was so lost in the groove of Ella Fitzgerald that a dirty bomb going off in the guest bathroom wouldn't have fazed her. They didn't see me come into the room at first, and I stopped, quietly, to watch them. They were so in love and so clearly happy that I wondered for a moment if Dad had been right that lying for the sake of good was the better idea over honesty. At least, until you fixed whatever you'd screwed up.

"Oh! You startled me. I thought our ghost was back," Mom said, clutching the glass necklace she'd made at an ashram in Tibet two summers prior. We'd never had a ghost, but for years Mom had insisted the humming sound coming from the refrigerator was the spirit of a Native American chief. After years of arguing that, no, that's merely what refrigerators sound like, I gave up and let her have her fantasy.

"Look at you. All cleaned up. What's the occasion?" Dad asked, big smile and no trace of panic whatsoever.

"I have a . . ." I felt my cheeks redden. Mom let out a loud squeal.

"You have a date, don't you?!" She clapped her hands excitedly, lowering the volume on the speakers. "Oh my stars! Our sweet boy has a date, Greg!"

This was exactly what I had feared would happen when I told them my plans for the evening. I had hoped I could slip out without much fuss, but seeing as this was nicest outfit I'd worn since, well, ever . . . it warranted an explanation.

"Greg, go get the camera!" Mom said, the beginning of tears forming in her eyes.

"Absolutely not," I said. "This does not require a camera, you guys. I'm just telling you where I'm headed." I took my keys off the counter, inching my way toward the front door, just as Dad returned with this old-school film camera and started snapping away like a paparazzo spotting a movie star eating a corn dog.

This was the perfect example of their overwhelming support. Supportive? Yes. Overwhelming? Very. It was never "have a nice time"; it was always "savor every minute, come home, write it all down, and turn it into something lyrical!" Life with my parents was like being trapped inside some art major's senior thesis and never being allowed to leave.

Mom and Dad forced their way behind me and snapped a photo of all three of us before I could shoo them away and get to the front door.

"I'll be home later. Okay?" I said, turning back to see their smiling faces watching me go. Despite their exhausting tendencies, it was impossible not to love those two weirdos.

# FRIDAY, SEPTEMBER 7, 7:01 p.m.

I CIRCLED THE BLOCK NINE or ten times because I'd arrived half an hour early. I hated being early, but I was afflicted by the disease of punctuality. This was likely attributed to the fact that for as long as I could remember, my parents had been the sort of people who seemed to make it their mission to be extremely late to *everything*.

"We're artists!" my mother would always say, an excuse she used for most things. No matter what the issue, being an artist seemed to be as good an excuse as any. Dropping me off an hour late to pretty much every day of kindergarten? Artists! Missing eight out of nine innings of my Little League games? Artists! Missing every flight to every city we had ever flown to? That's right, hand those rascals a paintbrush because they're artists!

One of my arguably pathetic forms of rebellion was that from the day I'd gotten my driver's license (an appointment we were late for because ARTISTS!), I had arrived way too early everywhere I went. The evening in question was no exception. However, this premature arrival could also be blamed on the excitement level of seeing Christopher outside of school in a situation that could potentially be considered a date if you were the type of person to consider that sort of thing a date, which I absolutely was.

"This is your first date," I said out loud to myself alone in the car, and quickly hated myself for doing so. "Get a grip," I then growled.

The radio repeated the same pop songs over and over, pop songs that were all about the same two things: either falling in love or falling out of love. Normally I might have spent the half hour contemplating why all these millionaire pop stars couldn't come up with something else to sing about, but that evening I had zero trace of snark or judgment. I seemed to have left my usual mind-set at home. This evening was a whole new me, a big smiling hopeful stupidly excited brand-spanking-new Marley, and as much as I hated to admit it, it felt pretty good.

Just then, someone blared a car horn behind me, snapping me out of my fog of optimism. When I started to honk back, I saw the adorable driver waving wildly at me through my rear-view mirror. He pulled up beside me in a very nice Mercedes. Apparently his father's infomercials had paid off.

"Hey! You're early!" Christopher said, like some overly cheerful waiter, in a way that would've normally annoyed me but with him, it warmed my heart.

"Oh, I just got here. I got a little lost," I lied, immediately wondering why I had done so but knowing full well it wouldn't be the last time I used a white lie to seem cool in front of him.

"Well, here I am to save you. Follow me, we'll park up the street."

He pulled ahead of me and I followed. I didn't believe it was possible to be saved by anyone, let alone some cute boy I'd only known for barely a week. But as I replayed his sweet little grin when he'd said "here I am to save you," I could think of only one thing:

*God, I really hope he does.*

Christopher's aunt Debbie lived in one of those cookie-cutter houses so packed full of stuff that you feel like you're inside a store with absolutely nothing you would want to buy. The place reeked of cigarettes, cat pee, and the sugary-sweet-smelling candles that were a blatant attempt to mask the two previous smells.

"Just so you know, Aunt Debbie is sort of the black sheep in our family. By which I mean, you're going to love her," Christopher whispered.

Aunt Debbie, as she insisted on being called by even those of us who weren't her nephew, was Christopher's mom's sister. She'd married some guy she met at a carnival on a whim twenty years ago, bought a house in Winston-Salem, and was promptly left for another woman a year later. As the abundant aroma of cat pee and cinnamon-roll-scented candles might indicate, Debbie had never remarried.

"Y'all get in there and get yourselves a plate before we run out of food," she said after we were introduced and I was instructed on what to call her. "Christopher can tell you how much food these folks can put away, can't you, sugar?" she asked, sucking on a cigarette and dropping ashes all over her filthy carpet without so much as a hint of caring.

Christopher and I exchanged bemused glances, his eyes seeming to say "we will debrief on Debbie later"—which was something I was very much looking forward to doing. I followed him out into the backyard, a veritable shrine to plastic pink flamingos and garden gnomes. The party was a mix of Debbie's friends, relatives, and coworkers from the local karaoke bar she managed (called, quite simply, Sing and Drink).

The crowd was a pretty rowdy group, lots of biker-looking men, and women who looked eerily similar to the biker-looking men, give or take a couple earrings. From the beer keg in the corner and the bottle of Fireball Whisky being passed around like communion wine, I could tell that Aunt Debbie didn't represent the conservative side of his family. I scanned the crowd, searching for his parents, and it wasn't long before my eyes fell on the reverend's toupee. Reverend Jim's toupee, in person, was truly one of the weirdest things I'd ever seen—and this is coming from a person who watched his mom perform a three-and-a-half-hour solo modern dance about how he was conceived. Standing next to the reverend was his wife, a woman so plucked and pulled by plastic surgeons it was a wonder she could talk.

"Can you guess which ones are my parents?" Christopher whispered in my ear with a perfectly devilish chuckle. "Oh, wave!"

He waved toward his parents, who were staring at us from across the lawn so disdainfully that it was as if we had walked into the party completely naked with the words GAY RIGHTS written on our bodies in pink lipstick. I gave them a timid wave as we made our way over to them. They gave me a historically dreadful stare back.

"Mom and Dad, this is Marley. Marley, these are my parents," Christopher said, bright and bubbly. Both his mom and dad smiled politely, the way politicians do when they see homeless people. Like, *I know I'm supposed to do something about this, but also ew.*

Up close, between the spray tans, Botox, and fake smiles, his parents looked bizarrely similar. Like those creepy twins in *The Shining* except not as cute and even deader in the eyes. They both seemed to exist in an unseen brittle and joyless bubble, the complete opposite of their free-spirited son. Compared to the rest of Aunt Debbie's friends, his dad was the most buttoned-up person in the history of buttons. When he looked at you, it wasn't AT you so much as through you. His smile seemed painted on and his teeth looked like a row of Altoids that had been hot-glued inside his mouth.

I could only hope his mom's hair was a wig, the kind of blonde and buoyant shape reserved for drag queens and country singers. She wore an expensive-looking skirt and jacket and smelled as if she'd bathed in perfume. Her makeup was so intense one could have mistaken her for a clown hired to make balloon animals . . . and she greeted me with all the sincerity of one.

"It's nice to meet you both," I said as politely as one can when speaking to people so politically opposed to you and how you were born that they've made millions of dollars off of it. My politeness seemed to put them off even more, so I was eagerly waiting for Christopher to break the awkward silence when Aunt Debbie barreled through with a tray of pigs in blankets.

"Wieners! Who wants a wiener?" she crowed before bursting into laughter so hard she almost dropped the tray. She looked at me and Christopher and said, "Probably don't need to ask you two, huh?"

The color drained out of the faces of Christopher's mom and dad—quite an accomplishment for two people as spray-tanned as they were.

"I'm going to get a Coke," I said, backing away from the powder keg of family dynamics as gently as possible.

Christopher caught up with me by the drinks table where I was pouring myself a cup of off-brand Dr Pepper called Professor Zest.

"Sorry to embarrass you—I should've warned you that Aunt Debbie loves to push their buttons." He threw a few ice cubes into his red Solo cup. "And I would apologize for them as well, but as you can see, they've built a career on being hopeless cases."

"Do they hate me?" I asked, feeling their vengeful gazes from across the yard.

"Probably." Christopher shrugged. "But don't pay it any attention. They hate everyone but Jesus."

The party slowly changed from an excuse for Aunt Debbie and her friends to binge-eat outside to an actual party. Thanks, in part, to the karaoke system set up in the corner of the yard, where Aunt Debbie was drunkenly belting her heart out to "Thunder Road"—but changing the lyrics to "Thunder Thighs" to decidedly cheap but rapturous laughter.

Christopher's parents had yet to say another word to me, or to anyone else for that matter. The more fun people had, the more put off they seemed to be behind their plastered fake smiles. It wasn't hard to tell that Aunt Debbie was taking great pleasure in her sister's and brother-in-law's discomfort. Christopher meandered around, demanding everyone put in song requests for karaoke. I had flat-out refused, and upon his mischievous reaction of "We'll see," I'd threatened all-out murder.

"C'mon," he said.

I informed him, "I categorize singing in public with wearing a Speedo. Why put myself or the world at large through that?"

He seemed to take the hint.

"Thank y'all! Thank y'all very much!" Aunt Debbie crowed over scattered yet rowdy applause. "While I'm up here and still sober enough to see, I'd like to toast y'all for coming tonight and for being in my life. It means a great deal to have each of you here. For different reasons." She put her hand on her heart, scanning the room, eventually landing her gaze on me. "Even you, Marley. Welcome to the family."

Christopher grinned at me as everyone turned their attention our way. His eyes were both flirtatious and apologetic. His parents looked as if they'd just realized their Diet Cokes were poisoned.

"Who's up next?" Aunt Debbie called out.

"Me!" Christopher shouted, strutting up to the stage like the kind of pop star who is so successful he has his own brand of electrolyte water and a pet tiger. Aunt Debbie whistled and clapped as she handed him the microphone.

"Well, first and foremost, let's all give the guest of honor a big round of applause and an even bigger happy birthday!"

Aunt Debbie basked in the cheering and applause before eventually batting it off. "Y'all calm down. It's starting to feel like you think this is my last birthday."

"Maybe your last as a *virgin*, Mary," Christopher teased with a crooked grin. The crowd ate it up—except for his parents, who put down their cups and started to gather themselves in a way that meant they were leaving the party *very soon*.

"You ain't too old for me to spank, mister!" Aunt Debbie bellowed with half a Miller High Life spilling out of her mouth and onto her ill-fitting sequin halter top.

"But enough about Aunt Debbie." He fastened the microphone into the stand. "This song goes out to that rare person you meet, out of the blue, when you least expect it. The one who you can just tell, right away, is really, really special."

He focused his eyes directly on me and I honestly thought I might pass out.

It wasn't until the music started that I realized the cutest boy I'd ever met was going to sing Katy Perry's "Teenage Dream" to me at his aunt's fiftieth birthday party . . . and I was somehow going to have to be okay with that.

Katy Perry is on the nose no matter the situation, but the one I was currently experiencing was a whole new level. This wasn't just cheesy; this was extra-large-Chicago-style-deep-dish-pizza-covered-in-mozzarella-Parmesan-and-crumbled-blue cheesy. This was the Cheesecake Factory and he was serving everything on the menu.

The one redeeming thing was that he was a terrible singer. Like, Audrey-level terrible. If he had started singing that utterly ridiculous song and sounded good, I think I would've had to turn around and leave the party.

Not only was Christopher a terrible singer, but he knew it. He *owned* it and was laughing at himself the entire time. Everyone watching was eating it up, with the exception of his parents, who were ignoring Christopher so strenuously you had to know they were hearing every word and knowing exactly where they were all directed. I couldn't help but relish in this understanding and be charmed by Katy Perry's bubble-gum-flavored lyrics for the first time in the history of my life.

Yes, it was stupid. Yes, he was making a total fool of himself. And yes, Katy Perry has had no business singing about being a teenager for at least two decades . . . but as I stood there in that backyard with that song going, the rest of the world seemed to fade away. It was just me and Christopher, laughing at this stupid song and, by doing so, feeling exactly what it was trying to say. We were seeing the world for how ridiculous it was and being the fools whose angst-fueled crushes made it so ridiculous in the first place.

As the song ended and everyone cheered, I looked over and saw Christopher's parents darting out to their car. Their faces had gone from orange to red with anger, and they hadn't even said good-bye to Aunt Debbie, who simply watched them go, shaking her head in unsurprised disappointment.

Christopher stepped off the stage and walked over to me.

"Guess my parents hate Katy Perry as much as you do," he said.

"How do you know I hate Katy Perry?" I asked, hoping I hadn't had some kind of frantic allergic reaction to garbage pop music and not realized it.

"Because you're far too mysterious and brooding to ever fall for her helium wiles." He leaned in close and whispered into my ear. "I've got you all figured out."

Unable to deal with his blatant flirtation, I did the only thing anyone would do in the situation—I walked over to get more cake. He laughed as he followed me, and I wondered if he just might be right.

Maybe, unlike me, he really *did* have me all figured out.


After we left the party, Christopher asked me to take him somewhere no one else would think to take him. It was a lofty request to put upon someone, especially in a small town like Winston-Salem, but I knew just the place. There was this old water tower a few miles out of town, out where Salem Creek dead-ended into what used to be a factory village but was now just a place for people to abandon old sofas and spray-paint curse words across the cracked pavement. It was the kind of creepy secluded place teenagers unanimously referred to as "The Spot," meaning the kind of spot teenagers go to smoke cigarettes and have their first kiss (preferably not at the same time). I'd spent my entire life dreaming of getting to kiss someone there. So in a moment of uncharacteristic decisiveness, I told Christopher to hop in and drove us creekward.

It felt surreal to have him inside my car. I drove silently, staring at the road, out of both my less-than-certain driving skills as well as not having any clue what to say. What do you say when you and a guy you barely know (but have already decided you've fallen in love with) are driving out to The Spot? Something like . . . "Hey, this is where a lot of people go to make out!"

I switched on the radio, which was turned up way louder than I had expected. Music began to shout at us, the speakers vibrating the car.

"Crap. Sorry!" I fumbled with the dials, lowering the volume to a reasonable level. "I don't usually listen to the radio."

"What do you usually listen to?" he asked.

"Nothing. I guess I like the quiet," I admitted, realizing how much of a loser I sounded like.

"Okay, then." He switched the music off.

"Oh, no. I didn't mean now," I said, turning it back on, the volume somehow having returned to that insanely loud level. I made a mental note to have my sound system checked out if I ever got a job/had money. "Jesus! How does that keep happening?"

He pushed my fingers away as I reached to lower the volume, and he turned it back off entirely. For that brief second where his fingertips were touching the back of my hand, I thought I might veer off the road and crash.

"You're right. The quiet is nice," he said, then remained quiet for a while. He was watching the passing road outside the window as I stole glances his way. The passing glow from streetlamps and fluorescent fast food signs lit his face in a multitude of colors, each one prettier than the last. Yellow from McDonald's, red from Chick-fil-A, purple from Taco Bell.

"So," he eventually said, "are you taking me to the woods to kill me?"

I laughed. It *did* seem a bit suspicious, the town disappearing little by little with each stoplight.

"This might be farther away than you had meant, but I promise it's worth it," I told him, wondering to myself if an abandoned water tower was in fact worth it.

"Okay, cool. But, like, you *are* taking me to the woods to kill me, right?"

I smacked his knee, then, in an act of extreme bravery, kept my hand there. He shut up for the rest of the drive.

✳    ✳    ✳

There was no one in sight at the water tower. Like a scene from an apocalyptic movie, all that remained were the crumbled remnants of brick factory buildings, heaps of litter, and the tall water tower with the rusted ladder crawling up its side. Beneath the tower was a big cement base where countless teenage dreams had become adult memories.

"This place is really cool," Christopher said, scanning the stretching field of nothingness. I sat and he stood at the base of the water tower. If you lay just the right way, you could see the most beautiful view of the mountains and a sky full of stars.

"I don't know if it's what you had in mind, but it's one of my favorite places. It's so peaceful. Audrey and I came here last summer when she made me take head shots of her to send in to audition for some shampoo commercial she read about online. I'm still not sure why we needed to be in an abandoned factory for a shampoo audition."

He picked up a rock and threw it across the parking lot, as if he were skipping a stone across a peaceful lake. It hit an empty glass beer bottle and shattered it, the sound echoing through the trees.

"Whoops." He turned back to face me with that devilish grin of his. "I can see myself liking North Carolina."

"Yeah?" I asked, attempting to contain the fact that this was quickly turning into the best night of my life. "Why's that?"

He plopped down beside me. "Oh, I don't know," he said ever so slyly. "I guess I just like the people I've met."

I could feel my heart inside my throat, or whatever it is that goes into your throat when you find yourself in the midst of a very emotional moment. This was one of the first times I could remember having this feeling, of choking but knowing you're not choking. You feel your neck getting hot and that same heat begins radiating up through your cheeks, to your temples and ears. If you're not careful, it will keep radiating upward until your eyes start to water and the whole thing becomes an unmanageable cryfest. Luckily, in this particular moment, I didn't let it get that far.

"I like the people I've met too," I managed.

"Oh really? Just in general? Like all the people you've met ever?"

"Oh God, no! I'd say it's the opposite, in fact."

This made him laugh really hard . . . and I hadn't even meant it to be funny. Making Christopher Anderson laugh was quickly becoming my favorite hobby of all time.

"Wow. Look at this view," he said, lying down and staring up at the mountains and the stars.

"It's nice, huh?" I lay down beside him, the skin on the back of my neck bristling from the cold cement. "When you get this far out of town, the mountain range is really something."

After a deep breath, he asked, "So, tell me, Marley. Are your parents as insane as mine?"

I wondered how that could even be possible but decided that wasn't the response he was looking for. I was being so careful with my words around Christopher and I was never careful with anything, especially not words.

"They are," I told him, "but in an extremely different way."

"How so?"

I went on to explain the history of my parents. How they'd met in college, moved to an artists' commune, traveled the world with a mime theater company, and became celebrated artists in their chosen creative fields all before I was conceived.

"Well, yes, I would agree that *is* indeed extremely different," he said with a snort.

"It can be intimidating, though," I rattled on. "They're *so* supportive, but that can be hard, trying to live up to their expectations."

"What are their expectations?" he asked.

"Me wanting something."

"And what do you want?"

"That's the problem—I don't know."

He rolled over onto his side, leaning on one scrawny arm, looking down at me. I could feel our hands on the pavement beside each other, just close enough to be touching but not.

After what felt like forever, he gently made them touch. Hold.

"You're seventeen. You don't have to know what you want yet," he said.

"What do *you* want?"

He bunched up his face and thought for a moment. "To change things," he said, followed by a hand slap to his forehead. "Oh gosh, that sounds so pretentious, doesn't it?"

From anyone else, yes. But that's the thing about when the person you like pays attention to you: They can be as pretentious as they want and you don't even notice.

"I just mean," he went on, "all the crap my parents have put me through and the kind of beliefs they spread around the world. They don't even realize how dangerous and damaging it is because they truly believe they're right. And they're not alone—the world is *full* of people like that. I'm lucky, because while sometimes it's really hard, I know that I'm strong enough to survive it. But a lot of people out there aren't. I guess I just wish I could do something to change all that. Also, I'd like to be a backup dancer for a pop star but I have literally NO rhythm."

"I know," I deadpanned. "I just heard you sing."

He rolled over, grabbing my shoulders, playfully shaking them. As he did so, our eyes met, and I saw the joy in his as he saw the joy in mine. Eyes locked in an almost surprised stare, seeing each other differently from this angle, our smiles mirroring each other like both sides of a heart-shaped locket, we were close enough that I could feel his breath on my face and he could feel my breath on his. The world went completely silent for that brief moment, and I knew that something very important was about to occur. I stepped out of my seventeen-year-old body and floated there above the scene, some version of myself I had yet to know. I remember it all. Every breath, every cricket's cry, every star, the cold cement, and his face as it floated down to join mine.

We kissed. Both sides of the heart-shaped locket fitting together perfectly.

We stayed like this, in our kiss, for a long time. Long enough that my legs fell asleep, and when we eventually stood up to walk to the car, I stumbled hard.

Christopher watched this with a hand to his cheek in disbelief.

"Can I say, I'm really glad that just happened," he said. "This night was beginning to feel far too perfect for you to be comfortable with."

I stood up and gave him the finger. He smiled and gave it right back.

It was official: Christopher Anderson and I were a match.

# SATURDAY, SEPTEMBER 8, 10:31 a.m.

MY PHONE DINGED, WAKING ME up. Which, aside from when my mom attempts to make gluten-free/vegan/raw pancakes, is the worst possible thing that can ever happen on a Saturday morning. I opened one eyelid, just wide enough to read my phone.

**That was really, really fun.**

Before I'd even gotten to the "topher" part of his name, I was sitting straight up, fully awake, and ridiculously cheery for a person who only moments before was in the midst of a delightful dream where he was swimming in a lake of birthday-cake frosting with a very friendly talking blanket. (There is no definition of this in my mom's dream dictionary, but I'm assuming it means something good.)

I held the phone in my hand, staring at the text, rereading it over and over. I had no idea what I was hoping to find upon a second, third, or twenty-ninth read, but that didn't stop me. I broke it down in my mind, word by word.

## THAT WAS REALLY, REALLY FUN.

THAT had suddenly become my favorite word. In that *that* he covered so much. The night, the karaoke song, the long drive out of town, The Spot, all those laughs, and, most important, the kiss. The kiss that had lingered on my lips for the past ten hours. The kiss that had prompted me to come home, take one look at myself in the mirror, and say out loud to no one in particular, "You're growing up, Marley."

My brain began to insistently wonder how one replies to the first text from his new crush. In my limited experience, it seems that when one begins to fall for someone, every part of their body falls for that person, but it's difficult to make every part of one's body agree on how to react. My fingers were eager to jump the gun and initiate a text conversation that would hopefully last until at least lunch. My brain wanted to wait, leave him hanging for a second, play hard to get, savor the thrill of his texting first for just a little while longer. My heart needed a second to process the past week, and my eyes were a little sore from the intense stare I had been giving my iPhone screen for the past five minutes.

I began to type.

**Me too**.

I immediately deleted this because it was lame and it also made no sense.

I began again.

**It was the best night I've had in a long time.**

I read this aloud to hear what it sounded like.

"Creepy," I said to myself, the delete button making its tapping sound with every dismissed letter. *Come on, Marley, it's just a stupid text message.* But we all know that it wasn't just a stupid text message. It was my *first* text message in our text thread; this text message would dictate the tone of our entire text conversation from now until who knew when.

I was racking my brain when I heard a door slam from down the hall. Then the stomping of feet. Then the opening of the just slammed door and my mother's yell.

"It's more than that, Greg, and you know it! It's about trust!"

Mom's voice was strained and angry, a tone it rarely took except when discussing gun laws or any form of music written after the mid-1970s.

"Sharon, if you'd just listen to me for one second without flying off the handle, I could explain," Dad begged in a tone not unlike a kid begging for a second ice-cream cone on a super-hot day.

The door slammed again, followed by the sound of my father's slow, dejected footsteps down the creaky floor of the hall, then out the front door. Then came that weird quiet that follows after two people have had a huge argument and everyone waits for someone else to pierce the uncomfortable stillness.

It was clear that Dad had broken down and told the truth. He'd confessed the news about the house and the debt. My parents rarely fought, so when it happened, it felt like the day-to-day rhythm of my life was somehow deceiving me. I felt helplessly like I should be helping, like when you know you should do some kind of exercise but you don't know what kind, so you just sit on the couch and watch TV for three hours (aka my every afternoon).

I had been so distracted by Christopher that it didn't really dawn on me until I was sitting there, everything silent except for the distant sound of Mom's muffled crying, that shit really had hit the fan. And life very well might be just about to change.

My phone dinged again. Another text from Christopher— this time an emoji smiley face. Despite everything that had occurred in the past few minutes, I smiled, just from thinking about him. I wanted to text back something that would continue the conversation but in a smooth, cool, totally non-desperate way. That, however, would require me to embody at least one of those three things, which was almost as likely as my parents eating at a KFC.

So I started with an emoji smiley face of my own. I couldn't believe I was allowing myself to turn into the kind of person who would send an emoji, let alone the one of the winking cat.


After avoiding it for a couple hours, I decided it was time to come out of my room. I was hoping I could sneak out the front door without having to confront what was going on. Dad hadn't come back and Mom had stopped crying a while ago, so I figured the coast was clear.

I opened my door very slowly, because when opened quickly the door would let out the kind of terrible high-pitched creak, more of a squeal really, that could be heard through the whole house and possibly next door. It sounded like a fourteen-year-old girl at the concert of her favorite boy band.

I quietly walked into the hallway, then turned the corner into the foyer of our house and put my hand on the front doorknob. Just as I turned it, I was startled by my mom's voice.

"Marley?"

I stopped and turned toward the living room, where Mom was standing on her head. Or rather, in "feathered peacock pose," which I recognized from the three years of "children's yoga" I'd been forced to attend back when most kids were learning how to ride a bike. By the time I had turned six I'd never played a video game but could recite almost all of the mantras by Bikram Choudhury.

"Oh, hi. What're you doing?" I asked, a pretty rhetorical question for someone standing upside down on a yoga mat and burning sage.

"What does it look like?" she asked. "Aligning my center and nurturing my core."

*But of course, Mom,* I thought but didn't say aloud. Instead I said, "Have you been out here long?"

"Only two and a half hours," she said, still upside down. "I hope you didn't overhear your father and me quarrel this morning."

It was stupid to pretend I hadn't. She knew just as well as I did how easily sound carried in our house.

"I did," I admitted. "Are you okay?"

She let out a very deep breath, the kind of deep breath you

can only let out if you've been upside down for two-plus hours and are still, shockingly, conscious.

"I'll be honest, Marley." She sat down in a cross-legged position. "I am angry."

I stifled a laugh, because even when professing her anger, my mom seemed calm and zen. Growing up, that had always made getting in trouble even scarier. There's nothing quite as spooky as accidentally breaking a super-expensive vase, then having your mother look at you, hold her hands together in prayer, bow her head, take a breath, and tell you, "I have never been more furious at a six-year-old in my life and I need to go outside to expunge this deep rage through dance."

"He told me that he already told you," she went on. "But I just want to say that I'm not upset with you for not telling me. I understand why you didn't."

I was off the hook on that front, a huge relief.

"He said he was trying to figure out how to fix it before he told you. Has he?" I asked. I could barely pass middle school math; I certainly had no clue how banking and real estate and mortgages worked. If I'm honest, I'm impressed that I even knew what a mortgage was at all.

"I saw the bills. He left them out on his desk and I went in there looking for my moldavite stones to bring into class. Do you know the biggest divine joke in all of this?" she asked, shaking her head at her own disbelief, as if to answer herself. "Moldavite is said to bring intense spiritual transformation."

She let out a "ha" and looked at me like she was asking, "Can you believe this?" I merely shook my head, hoping to rattle up a reply in there somewhere. I wasn't sure what kind of spiritual transformation losing our house would bring, and found it best to merely traverse ahead.

"So what now?" I asked.

"Now," she said, standing up slowly, stacking vertebrate by vertebrate like she taught her students to do, "we hope for the best, we try to fix it, and if we don't, then we don't."

"You mean if you don't, we lose our house?" I asked, attempting to make my personal panic subside. What did this mean for college? My future? And where would my parents live?

"Well, perhaps this is all some sort of sign. Like I said, moldavite is said to bring intense spiritual transformation. Perhaps this will be the transformation it brings."

"But, Mom—" I started, frustrated by her ambivalence. I wanted to demand she cry, freak out. That's what you're supposed to do in situations like this. Figure it out. Don't just let the universe settle things for you. Don't stand on your head for two hours, then give up. DO SOMETHING.

"But what, Marley? What else are we supposed to do?" she asked, looking directly into my eyes. I could see that behind her groovy demeanor was something far more real, or at least far more familiar: fear.

I swallowed whatever words I had intended to lecture her with next and merely shook my head.

"Whatever," I said, staring at my shoes. "I'm going to go for a drive."

# NOW

I WAS STUPID ENOUGH TO think I could scam my way into helping the world, helping Christopher, helping his parents and so many others to see what's right.

Harrison comes back into my dressing room, cradling four giant bottles of Fiji Water like someone holding infants who has no idea how to properly hold infants.

"Margaret Cho is running late. *Of course.*" He spits out his words like those frogs that spit poison. "So they're rearranging some things. The cast of *Wicked* isn't going to close the event—they're pushing them up and you're closing. I told them it would be suicide to close with a speech. Oh God, no pun intended."

He doesn't laugh, but I can tell that was his impulse. Harrison has made me hate sarcasm almost as much as I once loved it.

He looks at himself in the dressing room mirror, runs a hand through his perfectly coiffed hair, makes a duck face, then turns to face me.

"Hey, let's grab a selfie while we wait!"

I don't want to.

"Let's do it in the mirror; the lighting is gorgeous," he goes on, wrapping his arm around my shoulders and flashing a big, excited smile.

I join him. I hate myself, but I join him.

# SATURDAY, SEPTEMBER 8, 3:25 p.m.

SOMETIMES THERE IS NOTHING BETTER for the soul than going on a long drive all by yourself with your favorite playlist and no destination in sight. Ever since I'd turned sixteen and gotten my driver's license, this had been my favorite form of therapy. I found nothing more comforting than the open road. And comfort was definitely something I needed that afternoon; between the drama with my parents and the happiness of my night with Christopher, both my heart and mind were in the midst of a tug-of-war.

I pulled over and texted Audrey. And yes, I make an obvious point to mention that I pulled over to text because I make some pretty poor choices in this story, but texting and driving is not one of them.

**WHAT'RE YOU DOING?**

The little symbol indicating someone is typing popped up immediately.

When I got to Audrey's house, I found her wearing a silk kimono that would've seemed odd on someone else but on her just looked comfortable. She was the type of girl who wouldn't grow fully into her own until she'd tossed a martini into a man's face and said, "Take that, you bastard," before storming out of a penthouse.

It had just been Audrey and her dad ever since her mom passed away when we were in fifth grade, and while her dad loved her as much as a dad could love their kid, he basically let Audrey do whatever she wanted. This probably came from a combination of being overwhelmed by raising his daughter alone and the fact that Audrey was so bossy that even a decorated Navy SEAL would be terrified to cross her. She'd turned their house into a retired gay couple's Palm Springs villa full of vintage movie posters and antiques.

"I have Gruyère and Brie," she said, holding up two expensive-looking cheeses. "Which one would pair better with the blue?"

I shrugged. "Why not both?"

"I love the way you think, kiddo!" She delicately placed the cheeses onto her board of cured meats and olives. It was so nice it was almost restaurant quality.

We carried the plate of classy deliciousness into the TV room, where some old movie was playing on the screen.

"What're we watching?"

80

"*Torch Song*." Audrey squinted at the screen before finding the reading glasses she had taken to wearing on the end of her nose, glasses that I was 100 percent certain were just for show. "It's a moderately unknown Joan Crawford movie. I found it online. Besides the scene where she does blackface and ninety percent of the script and acting, it holds up."

I took the remote control and lowered the volume of Joan Crawford shouting an aggressively unmemorable song.

"Okay," I said, in that tone people use when they're announcing that they're on the verge of unleashing a solid five minutes' worth of talking and they don't want to be interrupted until they're finished. "So last night."

Audrey cocked her head to the side in confusion, then smiled.

"Oh, thanks for asking! It was great! Auditions ran long and I missed seeing the movie and I'm not sure if I'll get the lead in the show but I have a feeling I'll get one of the supporting roles. However, that is perfectly fine with me because the supporting role is where I can really shine. Steal the show and never give it back!" She rambled on. If I knew one thing about Audrey, it was that it was easier not to interrupt but to instead allow her to finish the story and pretend that something she'd said sparked whatever I was actually waiting to say myself.

"That's cool!" I said, as convincingly as one could without formal acting training. "That reminds me—my night with Christopher was pretty great."

"Oh, right!" Audrey popped a piece of Gorgonzola into her mouth. "Did you get laid?!"

I nearly spit out my Diet Mountain Dew. "Audrey!"

"Oh, *please*. Don't pretend to be a prude, darling. I've seen your web browser history."

"No. I did not *get laid*, as you so crudely put it. We had a really lovely time at his aunt's house. Then we went to The Spot."

Audrey contorted her face into a look of disgust. "You're telling me you went to The Spot and you *didn't* get laid? What's the point of going to The Spot, then?" She stuffed a few pieces of cured meat into her mouth, and I was relieved to see she'd be busy chewing for at least another thirty seconds.

"Because it was a quiet place to hang out," I said, as haughtily as Joan Crawford had just sounded on the TV when kicking a maid out of her dressing room. "Okay, we *did* make out."

"Aha! There's the story I'm looking for!" she shouted, flailing her arms around, the sleeve of her kimono slapping me in the face. "How was it? Good breath? Bad breath? Tongue? No tongue? Does he have all his teeth?"

"Good breath. He has all his teeth. And his tongue is none of your business."

"Okay, then, so yes. Tongue." She rolled her darkly lined eyes. "But wait, isn't he some kind of religious right-wing basket case?"

"His family is. He isn't," I quickly explained. "It's incredible. His parents have sent him to all these 'treatment retreats' and those horrible pray-the-gay-away camps, but he's not a rambling lunatic like you'd imagine. He's actually pretty secure and evolved."

"Wow," Audrey said, shaking her head with a hand to her heart. "I'd do *so* well in one of those camps. Everyone would be obsessed with me."

I decided it was best to ignore that comment, not because it was offensive but mainly because I was selfish and wanted to keep the focus on myself.

"Okay. Indulge me for a second," I began, sputtering my words as quickly as I could, humiliated to show my inner colors of desperation and borderline obsession. The way you rush through the story when you have to tell your parents you backed your brand-new Honda Accord into a Dumpster behind Rite Aid a week after getting your driver's license after the third time of taking the test. Not that I speak from experience or anything. "So. He texted me this morning, I texted him back, and then he texted me again, and I haven't replied yet. It's been over two hours. I want to write back but I also have no idea what to say or if it's too soon or—"

Audrey held up her hand, her face exhibiting the kind of expression you'd give a person with a clipboard on the street asking you to give them money to protect endangered fire ants.

"I do NOT like this age-appropriate demeanor you've started developing, my friend," she said with contempt in her eyes. "I don't like it one bit."

I felt not just my face but my entire skull blush.

"I know. I know. I am turning into the kind of person I hate. Not even hate—*loathe*. I feel like that time I tried tequila at Matt Robson's party and woke up the next morning in his parents' pool house in your skirt with dried Play-Doh stuck to my forehead with zero recollection of how I got there."

Audrey grimaced, remembering that chaotic evening.

"Seriously, Audrey. I don't know what's happening. It feels

like I got struck by lightning and electricity is buzzing through my veins and I can't make it stop. It feels like I could break out into song, and you know how much I hate singing. This is going to sound crazy, but I feel like I'm already falling for him." As I unloaded this monologue, my words sounded even more grotesquely precious out loud than they did in my head.

"After one date?" Audrey's tone was dry and mocking. "Why would that sound crazy?"

"Hey," I said, but I had nothing to follow it up with because she had every right to mock me. Hell, inside my own brain, *I* was mocking me.

But I also knew, with deep conviction, that Christopher was worth being completely and utterly on the nose for.

"I'm just kidding with you," she said. "I think it's really cool that you're experiencing this. It's about time you got out of your own head and let yourself be a stupid teenager. Go for it, darling."

She leaned back against the sofa, arms crossed, with a smile. I could tell she was genuinely happy for me.

"But promise me something," she added. "Don't ditch me in the process."

"Never!" I told her.

"Promise?" she asked, lowering her voice to what would have been a normal volume for most people but to Audrey was her version of a hushed whisper.

"I promise, dummy."

She smiled, and when she did so, I could see inside, past the self-constructed facade of the theatrical grande dame somebody to the insecure, gangly teenage nobody she really was.

Hanging out at Audrey's all day and talking over both Christopher and what was going on with my parents was just what the doctor ordered, but my mind couldn't pry itself from obsessing over when and what to text to Christopher next. I was new to text anxiety, which sounds more like the name of a terrible action movie and less like a real problem.

I racked my brain from the time I left Audrey's house and pulled into our driveway, my theory being that in the fifteen-minute drive I was sure to come up with *something*. Unfortunately, this had proven to be incorrect.

I decided it'd be best to leave it for one night and text him tomorrow.

The lights were on and I saw the silhouettes of both my parents through the window. I was dreading having to walk into whatever had transpired since the morning's dramafest but figured I might as well go ahead and rip off the Band-Aid.

The house reeked of sage, which wasn't necessarily uncommon. It usually suggested a special occasion, and when I turned to the living room and spotted my parents seated, holding hands, and chanting ancient Sanskrit aloud, I saw that this evening was no exception.

"Good evening, Marley," Mom said, looking up at me, her face smeared in lines of colored paint, something she'd picked up and racially appropriated from some ritual in some country I'd forgotten about her visiting. "Beautiful timing. Come, join us, we're healing."

Beautiful was not how I, personally, would have described this timing. Nor was I in the mood to partake in my parents' "healing" . . . but what else was new? I plopped down beside them; their faces shimmered with reflections of the messy pile of stones and crystals sitting before them.

"Marley, as you know, this morning, Greg and I were in the midst of a tailspin of negativity," Mom purred as she took my hand, each of us locking fingers with the person next to us, forming one of their little circles of enlightenment (their term, not mine).

"Sharon and I exchanged some charged words and negative energy." Dad squeezed both my and Mom's hands a little tighter with each word. "But we are here to release that deprecation."

"Let us conjure the gloomy auras surrounding this house, ourselves, our financial woes, our morning. Let us bring all dubious spirits into our realm. Let them hover here," Mom called out to the ceiling, as if it was going to answer her. The only difference between having parents who are extreme hippies and parents who are witches is that witches would actually *make* the ceiling talk, whereas hippies just like to stare at it.

They went through all their usual ritualistic antics: the chanting of mantras, the deep breathing, the offering up of our mistakes like sacrificial goats. I remained pretty tuned out but was happy to see that they were okay. Or rather, their version of okay.

As Mom began lighting the candles of peace, I asked, "So have you guys figured out what to do about the house yet?"

Both of their faces fell.

"Marley, this isn't about that. This is about healing." Mom glared at me, the flames from her peace candle lighting her from below.

"Houses are tangible, Marley," Dad said. "Money is tangible. We can only figure out the tangible details of life if we've figured out the bigger things first."

"But, you guys, the bigger things can't exist if we're suddenly homeless because you screwed up and lost our house!" I said, bold for once in my life.

"Marley, that is *not* the enlightened way to look at all of this." Mom's words were sharp and pointed, like the amethyst quartz scattered in front of her.

"Well, maybe we don't need to look at this with enlightenment," I snapped back. "Maybe we should be figuring out what the hell is going on and doing something about it!"

Both of their faces twisted into frowns of disappointment. They didn't shout back at me—that wasn't their way. That might have actually helped, might have at least made me feel like I was being heard.

"I think you should go upstairs and cool down," Dad said coldly. He didn't even need to finish his sentence, because I was one step ahead of him.

*       *       *

I couldn't stop thinking about Christopher's parents and the difference between them and my own. Sure, we agreed on very little. Sure, they preached some pretty harmful stuff. And sure, they fought against the acceptance of their own son so much that they were constantly sending him off to be "cured" . . . but, in my current state of annoyance, I couldn't help but respect that at least they fought for *something*.

Respect is a big word, I guess, especially when talking about two people who would likely rather I never existed at all than kiss their son.

I grabbed my phone and began typing a message to Christopher.

**Hey. Long day here. My parents are totally nuts. Kinda wanna crawl into a hole and sleep for the next year until I can move out.**

I sent it before rereading it, in my brave attempt to be unpassive, but I regretted it immediately. Before I could have time to completely hate myself, he responded.

**Join the club. I'm grounded.**

**Why?** I wrote back.

**YOU,** he typed, followed by an emoji with its tongue out, as if anyone would ever actually make that face.

**REALLY?** I asked.

**Wanna sneak out and meet me for fro-yo?**

This was literally all I wanted and hadn't even known it.

**YES!!!!!!** I wrote, then after a second thought, deleted the exclamation points and simply sent: **YES.**

Fro-yo (or frozen yogurt, as it used to be called before people found it too time-consuming to include those extra few letters) is the cheapest imitation of ice cream. Yet despite my strong views on this particular dessert front, I found myself sitting at the back table on the patio of Yogurt Time with Christopher, and I wouldn't have chosen to be anywhere else in the entire world.

"So then they sit me down in the living room, which is the one room of the house we never use. Wherever we are, they treat the living room like some museum for ugly furniture," Christopher explained through spoonfuls of white-chocolate-chip-covered yogurt. "So when they said they wanted to talk in the living room, I knew something was up."

He looked so cute in his T-shirt for a sports team I'd never heard of, his skinny freckled arms hanging out like sticks. I was trying really hard not to grin like an idiot.

"That's when they launched into their whole routine about how they're so worried about me and think I need more help and how they feel like they're failing as parents and blah, blah, blah," he went on.

"More help? Like more of that stupid camp?" I asked.

He nodded and rolled his eyes at once, teenage sign language for *my parents are douche bags.*

"Apparently some colleague of my dad's runs a 'retreat' an hour or so out of town. How convenient, huh?"

"What did you say?"

"I didn't say anything. I knew that if I did, they'd call me combative and out of control. That's what they always do. So I just sat there with my mouth shut, and when they finished the lecture I asked if I could go get some yogurt. That's one good thing about having parents who think you being gay is the end of the world—they don't worry about you going out late for frozen yogurt. My dad's just worried about his own reputation. People at his mega-church in Missouri flipped out when they heard I might be gay. It's one of the reasons we moved here, so God forbid that same thing happens again. Literally." He snorted at his own joke before going on. "I feel like a prick—I keep complaining about my life and you haven't gotten to complain about yours. And I know that's, like, your favorite pastime."

I could tell he was only half joking and liked that he already knew me well enough to do so.

"Shut up," I said, also only half joking. I could tell that he liked that he already knew me so well. "My mom found out about the house."

"Oh crap."

"Yep. Crap indeed. She and my dad had a big argument this morning—or quarrel, as they call it. For some reason they think the term *argument* is more destructive than the word *quarrel.*

These are the things they worry about instead of, oh, I don't know . . . paying for our home." I kept going. "So you would think that this would lead them to the first step in fixing the problem, right?"

Christopher shrugged his broad, bony shoulders.

"No. Instead I came home tonight to find them meditating with their crystals in the living room over their negativity toward each other."

Christopher pursed his lips, holding in a laugh like you would a burp when reading aloud in class, but he couldn't hold it in and burst out into a giggle fit.

"I'm sorry. Crystals?!" He choked through his laughter.

"Oh yes. Crystals. Not to mention prayer beads, dream catchers, and every other ritualistic device they can appropriate from other cultures to distract themselves from actually doing something about what's going on." I hadn't even touched my yogurt, so when I shoved a few spoonfuls into my mouth, it was more of a tart room-temperature soup.

"But they're not idiots, they can figure it out. Right?" Christopher said, more as a question than as a declaration.

It was my turn to shrug my less broad but still bony shoulders. We sat looking at each other for a while. Maybe it was just a few seconds, but in my mind it felt like forever because every thought I'd had all day disappeared as we sat there.

"Are y'all done with these?" an utterly joyless girl in a bright yellow Yogurt Time polo shirt and visor asked, appearing at our table with a tray and snapping me out of the dazed moment.

"Sure," I said, handing over my barely touched pool of melted yogurt and Christopher's completely empty bowl. The yogurt lady walked away without so much as a thank-you.

"Do you think it gets better?" Christopher asked, scratching his thumbnail across the tabletop, where generations of other teenagers in the same boat had scribbled their initials and various profanities, ancient cave drawings of students who had moved on. "You know, like they're always saying on TV and stuff?"

I didn't have an answer, certainly not the one he was hoping for, because I wasn't sure if it *did* get better.

"I don't kn—" I started before he cut me off.

"Yeah."

We sat staring at the table for a while. I could make out at least five obscene renderings of the male anatomy drawn with Sharpies.

"My parents just think the universe will fix everything," I said, without even meaning to.

"And mine just think that Jesus will," Christopher added, as much to himself as to me.

"But what if they don't? You know what I think? When you become a teenager, they should teach a class that tells you how much your life is going to suck. How much you're going to disagree with your parents, how lame school is going to seem, how stuck and alone you're going to feel as you wait for your life to happen. Because that's what being our age is like, isn't it? Just waiting for something, anything, to happen to us."

A mosquito landed on Christopher's hand and I instinctively smacked it. Its small black body oozed tiny drops of blood against Christopher's pale flesh like the first brush of color on a painting.

"Sorry," I said upon his flinch, grabbing a napkin and wiping off the nasty scene. As I did so, he took my hand into his and squeezed it tight.

"We have to *make* it better," he said. "You've talked a lot about a purpose or ambition or whatever you want to call it. But the only thing that we should really be worried about is making our lives into the lives we want them to be. Maybe things don't get better until we make them better."

I had never thought of it this way, but he was right. For the first time I felt something I'd only read about or seen in movies: hope.

"Let's make each other a promise," he went on. "It sounds stupid, but let's do that for each other: Let's help make things better."

"Okay. Deal."

"Or we die and get reincarnated into something with less crap to deal with," Christopher added.

I laughed.

"If you could come back as anything, what would it be?" he asked.

"I'm sorry, what?"

"I mean, it's silly, but, like, I always think about how when I die I hope I come back to life as a ladybug," he said, rolling his eyes before I could do it for him. "I know that's a ridiculous thing to say, but ladybugs get to be whoever they want and people don't care. In fact, people think they're cute. They're not even like other bugs. Nobody smacks a ladybug like you just did with that mosquito."

"Well, it was biting you," I said defensively.

"No, no. I don't care about that. I'm just saying, who doesn't smile when they see a ladybug? People just like them for who they are."

"I get it," I said. And I did. "Well, if you're going to be a ladybug, can I be a ladybug too?"

He grabbed my hand; his was cold from holding the cup of frozen yogurt.

"Absolutely."

We stayed like this—hands held, eyes locked, hope felt, ladybugs—until the place closed and the joyless fro-yo girl asked us to leave.

# NOW

I HAVE ALWAYS BEEN A pessimist. I always suck at sports because I just assume I will lose. I rarely study for a test because I figure I'll forget whatever it is I studied anyway. When I blow out my birthday candles I don't even wish, I merely wonder what stupid thing the universe will throw at me next.

There was such a large amount of optimism and kumbaya peace and love BS that my parents had shoved down my throat that by the time I developed thoughts of my own, I resented any kind of sincerity. But that's the world we all live in. Every blog, every tweet, every TV show, every headline is weighted in this disconnected sarcasm that has become the language of my peers. For some, it is just another passing fad. For others, like me, it gets in our blood and we stop seeing the world for what it *can* be but instead see it for what it *is*.

But do you want to know a secret? I have hated this about myself for as long as I can remember feeling it. But it's like that thing when you make a silly face and your teacher tells you to stop or else it'll stay that way. When you see the world through that negative lens for too long, it stays that way. You get stuck in a hopeless outlook that, sure, can make you and your friends laugh as you mock pop culture and whatever is seen as cool and trendy at that particular moment. However, I've grown to believe that way of thinking about or seeing the world destroys you bit by bit without you even noticing. You can't only see and joke about what's wrong; you also have to force yourself to stop and look around. Then, once you've done that, fix what you see is wrong.

That's what Christopher did for me. For the first time in my life I stopped and saw the world as something other than a constant punch in the gut. And as we laughed together, shared secrets, and dreamed about a better tomorrow, it wasn't just the first time in a long time I'd encountered the strange feeling of hope; it was also the first time in forever that I was making someone else feel it too.

This is an intoxicating feeling. And like all intoxicating things, it's fun until it's poisonous . . . and usually you realize that just before it's too late.

# FRIDAY, SEPTEMBER 14, 3:15 p.m.

THE GOOD NEWS WAS THAT a week had gone by and the world hadn't ended. The bad news was that Mom and Dad appeared to have zero plans for how to save our house and Christopher's parents had taken away his phone and grounded him from socializing outside of school after they found out he'd had frozen yogurt with me.

Audrey had gotten the role of Cinderella's Stepmother in the school production of *Into the Woods*—which, based on Audrey's reaction, was the worst news of all. She wouldn't have any song of her own or any real moment to shine. Instead, she swore, she'd do what all great actresses do and conjure everything in her power to steal the audience's attention in every scene despite her role not being important. I didn't have the heart or energy to explain to her that I was pretty sure that's *not* what great actresses do.

There are few things worse than really liking someone and then suddenly being forbidden to see them. Even if you've only known that someone for less than two weeks.

Lunchtime had become these little half-hour binges on all things Christopher. Over our room-temperature teriyaki chicken bowls, we'd barely have time to breathe in between stories of everything from what I'd watched on Netflix the previous night to what kind of shampoo he was currently using to the fact that we'd both dreamed of each other every night since our kiss at The Spot.

By the middle of the week it had become clear that seeing each other for just those thirty short minutes a day was only going to drive our angst-fueled teenage hearts into hysteria. I devised a plan for both of us to sign up for the tech crew of *Into the Woods*. Christopher's parents wouldn't forbid him from participating in after-school activities even though painting the trees for an amateur production of a Stephen Sondheim musical might be the only thing gayer than sneaking out to meet your boyfriend for frozen yogurt.

The plan worked and the crew had its first session Friday afternoon. Mrs. Reichen, a parent volunteer who seemed way over her head and genuinely terrified by her leadership position, had instructed us to bring 1) a pair of clothes we wouldn't mind getting paint on and 2) a good attitude. With an old pair of Dad's overalls, I was good for one of the two requests.

The crew members that assembled were a ragtag team of peers who had nothing better to do on a Friday afternoon. It was comforting to be around so many of my lost brothers and sisters. Christopher waved at me from across the room as I snuck in a few minutes late, just as Mrs. Reichen began her welcoming speech.

"Thank you so much for signing up to help out with the set of the fall production of *Into the Woods*." Mrs. Reichen's voice trembled with anxiety, as if she were being forced into this volunteer set-painting experience at gunpoint. "I'll be filling in for Mrs. Watson, whose knee injury has made her unable to help out this year. This is my first time leading so many people, so . . . be nice!" She forced out a giggle that all but shouted desperation.

Christopher and I met each other's glances, immediately having to stifle laughs.

"So . . ." She read from a xeroxed sheet of directions that was shaking in her sweaty hands. "Get a partner and grab two brushes from the paint closet located backstage left. Please do not let the students be alone with any spray paint or other aerosol products—oh, I'm not supposed to read that part." She bowed her head in humiliation.

Christopher and I buddied up and joined the line outside the paint closet.

"It's cool they hired a woman on the verge of a nervous breakdown to supervise us," I observed. "How are your painting skills?"

Christopher shrugged. "I don't know. I can't even remember the last time I painted or drew something. Probably not since that time my parents took me out of second grade to help them make protest signs to hold outside an abortion clinic."

"Naturally." I handed him a brush and grabbed one for myself, walking back toward where Mrs. Reichen was pacing around the canvas flats laid across the stage. Christopher grabbed my wrist.

"Hey. Wait."

I turned to face him just as he planted a kiss right on my lips.

"I've missed you," he told me.

My spine quite literally tingled.

"I've missed you too," I told him back.

With the sound of the cast rehearsing "Children Will Listen" in the next room, the moment felt as close to perfect as moments could get.

"Get a room," a kid whose face looked like a thumb chuckled as he walked by us. I blushed and followed Christopher to the stage.

We spent the next two hours of "crew" laughing at and teasing each other, while painting the canvas flats white. We were covering up the set from last year's production of *Fiddler on the Roof*, and there was something slightly discomfiting about painting over a Jewish village after having watched it be invaded by Cossacks in the year prior.

We wrote secret messages to each other—*I like you* and *follow me into the woods* and *we might not be home before dark*. Then our words would vanish to the naked eye as we painted over them. But we'd still know they were there.

Eventually the rehearsal ended and the backdrops were as white as they needed to be. Mrs. Reichen dismissed the crew, which meant Christopher and I had to say our good-byes in the hallway outside the auditorium.

"When do you get your phone back?" I asked, attempting to hide my desperation for an answer like "tomorrow."

He said he didn't know.

"This is so weird, isn't it?" I added.

"What? Not being able to talk to each other, or falling so massively, completely, and utterly for somebody?"

He was *so* smooth, melting my heart before I even realized it. He grinned, knowing how smooth he was and how effective it was on me.

"Well, both," I sputtered.

"Yeah. Both." He pulled me into his chest. He smelled like detergent, sweat, and paint. "Hey. Want to go to the fall dance with me next weekend?"

He gestured over to a stupid-looking poster where two leaves were dancing arm in arm, surrounded by music notes.

"But you're grounded. Will your parents let you?" I asked. I had never even been to a school dance, for many reasons.

First, I'd always found group activities to be trite and exhausting.

Second, I had never been invited.

"I don't know," he said. "But I'll figure something out. How many chances do you get to go to your high school fall dance?"

I began to point out that the answer would be, quite simply, four . . . but I bit my tongue so I wouldn't look like a dick and ruin the moment.

"Well, four, I guess," he added, and I beamed at this glint of sarcasm in the midst of his earnestness, which had quickly become one of my favorites of his traits. "What?"

I shook my head, my grin stretched so wide it almost hurt.

"I just like that we're on the same page," I said.

His grin mirrored mine. "Me too. Which is how I'll figure out a way to get there." He squeezed my hand. "Okay?"

"Yeah," I breathed. "More than okay."

We kissed good-bye. Then I went back to my car and felt the Christopher-shaped absence in the seat next to me. I had no doubt it would follow wherever I went, until he and I could be in the same place again.

# SATURDAY, SEPTEMBER 22, 10:45 a.m.

IT WAS A LONG WEEKEND of not knowing what he was doing. Then I got to school on Monday and found a long letter waiting for me, telling me not only about his weekend but about his life before. This set the story line for the whole week—when we weren't talking at lunch or cavorting over canvas backstage, we were writing down our lives for each other. Not texting. Not emailing. Actually writing it down, the handwriting as intimate as his voice in my ear. I learned how he first realized he was gay when watching Zac Efron in *High School Musical 3* for the first time, a sincerely game-changing experience for any teenage boy or girl with an affection for boys. And how the first boy he liked turned out to be straight and made out with him in the school supply closet anyway but promptly punched him in the face a week later.

We got to know each other. And we each got to know what it felt like to be known, and to want to be known.

On Friday, he vowed that he'd make it to the fall dance. (*I won't leaf you stranded on the dance floor* were his exact words.) As soon as I left school, I sent out a code red to Audrey regarding what the hell I was going to wear. She had a good eye for finding the hidden treasures in thrift shops and other places that fit my limited budget. Likely because "thrifting" had been Audrey's favorite hobby since she was a pillbox-hat-wearing eleven-year-old.

As long as I put my foot down when she tried to put me in ascots and smoking jackets, I could always count on Audrey to guide me through any fashion emergency.

We'd made plans to meet at Second Time Around Thrift Shop at ten on Saturday morning, which, knowing Audrey, actually meant ten thirty, and by a little after ten forty-five she finally arrived with her usual giant Starbucks cup wearing a not-as-usual-yet-not-uncommon gold turban. (She'd stopped wearing said turban to school when the faculty had established a no-hats-of-any-kind policy. This policy came after Audrey took to showing up every day in an enormous hat she'd worn in a community theater production of *My Fair Lady*. The hat in question was so big people had to duck away from its path as she walked through the halls.)

"This is the earliest I've been up on a Saturday since I stood in line for Idina Menzel concert tickets!" she shrieked from across the parking lot. "Christ knows, I hope this proves to be a better all-around experience than *that*."

She'd dragged me along to said Idina Menzel concert, which turned out to be a real disaster from the moment she walked onstage and announced she wouldn't be singing *any* show tunes of *any* kind and instead her "original pop stuff." I've honestly never seen an angrier mob of gay men in my life, and I saw that movie about Stonewall.

"Good morning, darling." Audrey greeted me with her usual kisses on both cheeks. "What are we thinking? Black tie and tails?"

She was already pushing through the revolving door into the thrift shop before I could protest.

"No! It's the fall dance, not the Oscars, Audrey," I said once I'd caught up with her. "It's, like, not as dressy as prom but still dressy. What's that called?"

"Lazy," she fired back, grabbing a tuxedo jacket the color of dried vomit and holding it up to my face. "If this were your color, it'd be fabulous."

"I don't think that thing is *anyone's* color." I shuddered, hanging the jacket back on the rack, where it would probably stay until someone needed something to wear when they went as "pure garbage" for Halloween. "I'm thinking a nice dark jacket and a T-shirt. But a nice T-shirt."

Audrey rolled her eyes as she sorted through the rack of dark-colored sport coats. "I doubt Cary Grant ever even said the words *nice* and *T-shirt* in the same sentence," she mumbled under her breath. This was one of her go-to arguments against a thing she didn't approve of, comparing it to how a classic movie star would've felt about it. She'd once asked a completely boggled Subway employee if she thought Greta Garbo would've wanted "extra mayo" on *her* veggie sub.

"How are you two even pulling this off?" she asked. "I

thought he'd been grounded by baby Jesus or something." She examined the label of a jacket, then put it back in horror as soon as she saw the word *Sears*.

"I don't know. I'm just supposed to meet him at seven in the gym. He said he would figure out how," I told her. I was more than a little nervous that this entire plan would end in my pathetically standing in the gym at my first high school dance, waiting, unsuccessfully, for my date to show up.

"While I might be shocked, I am rather proud of you for agreeing to go to something as ridiculous and frivolous as a school dance," Audrey said, dumping a stack of jackets into my arms and leading me to the pants section.

"Um. Thanks?"

"No, no. I don't mean for that to sound as backhanded as it does. I just mean it's nice to see you excited about something. It's very un-you." She narrowed her eyes at me and smirked. "You really like him, don't you?"

I thought about his smile, his laugh, his smell, his chin, his nose, his eyes . . . and simply nodded. Just then Bernadette Peters began singing from inside Audrey's purse.

"Who would be calling me from Missouri?" she asked, fishing out her phone and skeptically staring at its screen.

"Missouri?!" I fired back. "Christopher is from Missouri!"

"Okay, well, I doubt very seriously your boyfriend is calling me at eleven on a Saturday morning." But she went ahead and answered. "Hello?"

Her eyes widened.

"Hi." She mouthed the words, *You're right.*

"Wait. It's Christopher? What does he want?" I whispered. "Don't tell him we're buying me an outfit at a thrift store! He drives a Mercedes."

"Oh. Wow. That's . . . I mean, I hadn't planned on it." She paced around the pants section. "But . . . okay. I think I'm picking up on what you mean and, fine, I'll see you at seven."

She hung up.

"That was Christopher?" I asked.

"Yeah."

"What did he want?"

"To ask me to the dance."

I nearly dropped my stack of secondhand outerwear. "Wait. WHAT?"

"It isn't like that. Clearly. I could tell from the lilt in his voice. I can spot a terrible actor from miles away," she explained, relishing in her solving of a mystery. "He said his parents had reconsidered his grounded status after he'd told them how much he wanted to take this girl Audrey to the dance. Don't you see? I'm the decoy to get him to you. If it weren't so Shakespearean, I'd be deeply offended."

I was impressed at his craftiness, let alone at his ability to track down Audrey's number. Was it sad he had to lie in order to see someone he liked? Sure. But if it was the only way to get him to the dance, then it would have to do.

"So you're going to come?" I asked, hopefully and apologetically all at once.

"Now, most importantly, what will *I* wear?" She was off to the rack of slightly stained evening gowns before I could even thank her.

Audrey and I got ready together at her house over a bottle of room-temperature champagne she'd stolen from her father's liquor cabinet. I didn't know enough about champagne to know whether or not the fact that it tasted like soap meant it was good or bad.

After what had turned into a three-hour shopping experience, Audrey had settled on a floor-length crushed-velvet sleeveless gown, which was already way more formal than anything anyone else would be wearing. Then she added satin gloves that went halfway up her arms.

"Tell me the truth—would this tiara be too much?" She held a sparkly rhinestone tiara that was most definitely too much up to her head.

"Yes," I said as firmly as cement.

She didn't object and continued to apply her makeup, something between elegant and full-blown drag queen after too much chardonnay.

"Can you tie this?" I asked, wrapping the tie Audrey had insisted I wear around my neck. We'd made a deal: I could wear jeans if I wore a tie, a peace treaty in accessories. My father had tried to teach me how to tie a tie on numerous occasions, but despite that and watching a few YouTube tutorials, I'd never mastered it.

"Darling, we simply *must* get you sorted out someday," she said, clenching her teeth for effect, and perfectly tying the stupid thing in no more than ten seconds. "Now. How do we look?" We both turned to look at ourselves in the mirror. We looked nice. Classic and borderline great.

"You look beautiful," I told her, and I meant it. Audrey was genuinely beautiful, but the kind of beautiful that wouldn't be appreciated until she got out of a small town.

"Oh stop," she argued, pursing her lips together and snapping a selfie quicker than you could say "vanity."

"Hey. Thanks. I know this is gross," I said to her reflection. She turned away from the mirror and faced me. Our reflections seamlessly shifted to genuine eye contact.

"What is?" she asked.

"This. You pretending to be my boyfriend's date so we can go to the fall dance," I explained. "It's like one of those bad nineties gay movies we never watch on Netflix. I'm sorry it had to be this way, but I hope you know how much this means to me."

Audrey's cartoonish red lips turned up into a caring smile. "Darling. You are my best friend. And I would lie down in traffic for you if it came to that. I mean, as long as I wasn't in Chanel."

I laughed and grabbed her hands. We stood there, hand in hand, staring at each other like two people in love. Because we were in love and had been since the day we met. A different kind of love, but a definite and most certain love.

"It's just so cliché, the straight-girl best friend without a date going to the dance as a ruse for—"

She held up her freshly manicured hand for me to stop. "It *is* cliché. But you know what, Marley? Some things are cliché for a reason. From Harper Lee and Truman Capote to Will and Grace to Andy Cohen and Sarah Jessica Parker. I'm *proud* to be your friend and fight for you, and if that makes us cliché then so be it," she said with her glittering green eyes locked on mine. "And besides, I could have a date if I wanted one, but you know how much teenagers depress me. That said, look at what I'm wearing . . . something tells me that by the end of the night, I'll have more than one."

I pulled her into me and hugged her tight.

"I'm so lucky to be your friend," I whispered into her overly perfumed neck.

"Oh, calm down. You know I detest this sappy version of yourself that love is turning you into." She pecked a small kiss on my cheek, small enough to not screw up her makeup. "Now shut up and latch these pearls."

# SATURDAY, SEPTEMBER 22, 7:01 p.m.

THE PLANNING COMMITTEE HAD DECORATED the gym in an autumnal theme so tacky it was almost pretty. Bales of hay and pumpkins lined the walls, artificial leaves hung from the basketball nets, and the sweet smell of apple cider filled the air. September had always been the month they hosted the fall dance, which might have made sense before global warming but now only served as a grim reminder that the earth is on fire.

We had arrived right on time, so Christopher wasn't there yet and the place was half empty, giving us a chance to do what we did best: Scan the room and judge what everyone was wearing.

"I will never understand poly-cotton, and the same can be said for gingham," Audrey hissed as an extremely pretty girl in an extremely tacky dress walked by with her extremely handsome date. She continued. "That's the thing about being beautiful and popular, though—if you're not careful, it encourages you to be basic and unstylish."

The DJ was playing an assortment of parental-advisory-board-approved Top 40 songs, which limited the selection to more like Top 22. Only a handful of people were dancing; most were hanging to the sidelines with cider and the one-of-a-kind awkwardness of teenagers in formal wear.

"This is going to be a long night. Get me half a cup of cider, will you?" Audrey asked.

"Half?"

"Sure. Need to leave room for this." She revealed a flask hidden in her clutch.

Before I could walk over, I felt a tap on my shoulder. I turned around and was face-to-face with Christopher. His usually messy hair was slicked back like he was someone who manages a bank, and he was wearing a slightly too big navy-blue blazer, a white button-up shirt, and a red, white, and blue tie. Forget the bank—he looked like he was ready to run for Senate.

"Hi," I said, flustered.

"Well, hello," he said, smooth.

We must have looked pretty silly because Audrey rolled her eyes and growled, "Oh, forget it. I'll help myself," then proceeded to make her way over to the refreshments table.

"You made it." I hated the stupid smile I could feel across my face. "How did you even get Audrey's number?"

"The *Into the Woods* cast and crew contact list," he said. "Duh."

Duh indeed.

"And your parents bought it?"

He grinned. "I should be *starring* in the school play, not painting the set. You should've seen my act. I sat them down, I fought back tears, I told them I needed to confess something, and then went into this whole monologue about how I had met a girl and thought I might be cured of my homosexual affliction. That's their term, by the way—doesn't that make being gay sound like a podiatry infection?"

"Did you feel bad? Lying to them, I mean?" I asked, wondering to myself why I cared.

"Are you kidding?" He scoffed. "After everything they've done to *me*? Besides, it's a white lie. White lies are good sometimes."

"I can't believe they just immediately bought it. How was it *that* easy?"

"Because it's what they *wanted* to believe. That's the thing about people like my parents—they're aspirational thinkers. Maybe everyone is. As long as it fits into the narrative they're after, then it's more than welcome. Isn't that depressing?"

"Very."

"Now, enough about my parents. Let me take a good look at you."

He stepped back, examining me up and down. His utmost attention turned me into a cheap imitation of Bashful from *Snow White*.

"Stop. You're making me feel stupid." I playfully pushed him away.

"You are the most handsome guy I've ever seen. Do you know that?" he whispered in my ear as he pulled me into him.

And I thought, yeah, little white lies aren't *that* bad.

"So," he continued, "what does one do at a school dance?"

I shrugged as Audrey appeared beside us with three spiked apple ciders and the answer to his question.

"First," she said, "I'm taking an adorable picture of the two of you. Then we toast. Then we dance. Then, later, I screw off so you guys can make out." She passed out the cups. "To fighting for what you want. Even if it's just the chance to dance with a cute boy at the school gym."

"Hear, hear!" Christopher cheered, clinking his plastic cup against ours.

As the dance wore on, the music shifted from loud headache-inducing dance beats to the type of mellow songs that are specifically written for slow dancing in high school gymnasiums.

Audrey hadn't properly paced herself as far as the boozy cider was concerned and had taken over emceeing the evening, a position originally held by a perfectly nice but charisma-challenged sophomore from the planning committee. Audrey had literally ripped the microphone out of her hand.

"Let's hear it for all the lovers here tonight, ladies and gentlemen." Audrey slurred like a cruise ship singer asking if anyone is from out of town. A few kids clapped and cheered with the enthusiasm of people watching a documentary on the history of copper. "I'd just like to say, on behalf of our entire class, that this has been one of the best fall dances in the history of the school!"

Anyone who had attended the previous fall dances could have pointed out that Audrey had in fact never been to one, but the line got her a round of applause nonetheless.

"She's a real natural, isn't she?" Christopher said quietly.

"A natural what?" I replied.

"Zing!"

"Maestro, if you please, a little something slow!" Audrey shouted at the DJ as if he were a twelve-piece orchestra. "This one goes out to my best friend . . . you know who you are."

Christopher squeezed my shoulder as we took each other's hands and began dancing to the sweet, slow song. Can we all just acknowledge that slow dancing is incredibly awkward? Our bodies are not used to moving that slowly, and certainly not while holding on to another human being, and most certainly not while in a gymnasium filled with our peers. Regardless, I was savoring every moment and lost in a trance.

"Faggots," a mid-pubescent voice squeaked from beside us. The squeaky vulgarity was coming from a pimply-faced freshman slow-dancing so far apart from his date you could have built a condominium between them. The girl snickered, the way girls do when stupid boys make stupid jokes and they feel obligated to laugh at them.

"Ignore it," I whispered as Christopher's face twitched in the kid's direction. "He's just a kid."

"So are we," Christopher objected, with an air of sadness.

"Yeah, but he's an idiot. Don't let him ruin our night," I said.

Christopher took a deep breath and we kept dancing. I took his chin in between my fingers, shifting his face to look at mine. I made a really stupid face to make him laugh. He did.

"Oh, did I hurt your faggot feelings?" the kid egged us on with a sneer.

We stopped dancing and I tried pulling Christopher off the dance floor.

"Let's just get some more cider," I said, tugging on Christopher's arm.

"What did you say to me?" Christopher demanded, twisting out of my clutch.

In one quick move, Christopher had the kid by the collar. The kid looked scared as Christopher towered over him.

"Come on. Just let him go," I said. "It's not worth it."

"Listen to your little boyfriend, fag," the kid said from within Christopher's grip, and that's all it took. Everything slowed down. The music seemed to fade into a long droning sound as Christopher flung his arm way back, clenched his hand into a fist, and smacked the kid right in the cheek with a loud, pounding boom. The kid fell back, tripping on his own feet onto the floor, as everyone around us gasped.

"STOP!" The squeaky kid's date shouted loud enough for everyone to turn and look. Suddenly, teachers and chaperones came rushing over. Taking one look at the short bully on the ground, two grown-ups pulled Christopher away like he was the bad guy.

"Christopher!" I called out as the two teachers dragged him through the forming crowd. "Let him go! It wasn't his fault!"

But it was too late; he was gone, carried off to the principal's office, the strangest place to be on a Saturday night.

# NOW

WHEN YOU'RE A GAY KID, you get used to the name calling. You get used to the cruel comments made by peers and teachers and people's parents and on TV. It never ceases to sting, but we build our shells so the words won't break us. We create our armor for the battle to be the person we were born to be. For some it's toughness, for some it's creativity, for some it's drag, for some we're still figuring it out. It can be anything. Maybe that's why gay people are so strong.

For me, it had always been the ability to tune it out, to ignore it the way my mom ignores it when my dad farts at the dinner table. For each of us it's different, but that night was the first time I'd seen someone's shell crack open and watched someone stand up for himself in the face of a bully. In a lot of ways, that night was the beginning of the end for my shell. It would be a while before it shattered completely, but looking back, I can see now that watching Christopher defend us that night was the first crack that led to all of this.

# WEDNESDAY, SEPTEMBER 26, 7:46 a.m.

I HAD GOTTEN TO SCHOOL early for the past three days and waited by Christopher's locker, in the event that he showed up. I hadn't heard from him since the dance and he hadn't come to school. I'd tried to follow him to the principal's office Saturday night but they wouldn't let me. I assumed they'd called Christopher's parents. Which would mean that his parents had found out who he'd been dancing with when the altercation had occurred. Which would mean who knew what for where Christopher might have been at that particular moment.

Audrey had tried calling for me a few times, but Christopher's parents had hung up on her as soon as she said her name. The jig was up. I had spent the past three days feeling so depressed that when I was at home I'd stayed in my room, avoiding my parents at all costs. I didn't want to burden them with my own drama in the midst of theirs.

Part of me was wishing Christopher hadn't stood up for us. If he hadn't, he wouldn't have hit that kid, and if he hadn't hit that kid, our night could've ended like I'd imagined: eating fast food and making out by the water tower. (Maybe not in that order.)

But it's that kind of attitude, I reckoned, that kept bullies bullying and the homophobes of the world staying the same. Christopher had done the right thing; I just resented the universe for the fact it had ruined our perfect night.

I waited by his locker for a full hour, making the last-minute decision to skip homeroom altogether, but he never showed up. I had tried to remain hopeful, but after three mornings of no sign of him, I had the overwhelming sensation that something was definitely wrong.

By biology class, he was still nowhere in sight, and he didn't show up to lunch either. I had asked around to people I recognized from his classes all week, each of them looking at me like I was some kind of spooky stalker. They all said the same thing: *Haven't seen him.*

By the end of the school day I was at a "someone realizing they left their curling iron on and sitting atop a box of tissues for three hours" level of panic. I tracked down Audrey outside on the quad, where she was taping *Into the Woods* posters to all the trees.

"Isn't this neat? Posters for *Into the Woods* on wood. Clever, huh?" She smirked proudly.

"What do I do?" I asked. She didn't have to ask what I meant, as my question was a continuation of the endless text conversation I had kept Audrey locked into all day.

"Don't panic. Maybe he's sick."

"Come on. He's not sick. Something's definitely up."

Audrey sighed. She knew I was right. She gave me a big, tight hug that cracked my back.

"How about this? I'll drive us by his house and we can see if his car's there," she offered.

It was a drastic move, and a little more Nancy Drew than I was imagining . . . but it gave me an idea of my own.

The doorbell at Aunt Debbie's house chimed out Elvis Presley's "Can't Help Falling in Love" in a series of shrill beeps and dings that sounded more like a failing heart monitor than the iconic pop tune—followed by the meowing cries of her veritable pride of stray cats.

"Are the cats part of the doorbell, or are they real?" Audrey asked.

"They're real. *Very* real," I grimly offered.

"Please, whatever happens to me, never let me turn into a cat lady. I'd rather be one of those people they do half-hour reality shows on about being addicted to drinking lighter fluid or eating the stuffing from their sofas. Just not cats."

Aunt Debbie wasn't answering the door and there was no car in her driveway. It had been a long shot, but I knew that if anyone in Christopher's family would tell me what was going on, Aunt Debbie would.

"She's not here. Let's go." I sighed, just as her bumper-sticker-covered, dented powder-blue Chevy Malibu came pulling up the gravel driveway.

"Hey, cutie pies!" Aunt Debbie crowed, rolling down her window.

She parked and got out of the car, lugging more than an armful of cat food.

"You wouldn't mind grabbing the rest out of the trunk, would you?" She motioned back to the car as she breezed past us.

Audrey and I opened her trunk to discover even more cat food. Audrey was visibly shaken.

"Promise me," she hissed under her breath.

"I promise."

Aunt Debbie was already pouring the dry kibbles of food into the bowls scattered throughout the living room when we came in.

"Just sit those anywhere. Thanks, baby dolls. I'm Debbie, by the way." She reached her hand out to Audrey, who shook it tentatively.

"Audrey. Charmed to meet you."

Aunt Debbie pursed her lips. "Charmed? How fancy. You from over there in Europe or something?"

"She wishes," I said. "Christopher wasn't at school today and something happened over the weekend at the fall dance and I'm worried something is wrong."

Aunt Debbie lit the cigarette she had been holding in her mouth since she pulled up, then frowned, immediately dropping it onto her shag carpet.

"Shit!" She stomped out the glowing ash beneath her foot. "Well, I'm glad you came by because I didn't have a clue how to find your address."

"My address?"

She walked over to her purse and began rummaging through it, pulling out an assortment of things a sane person would have simply thrown away: empty cans of Sprite, a Ziploc bag of stale-looking Fruity Pebbles, and finally . . . an envelope.

"Here it is." She handed it to me. "He slipped it to me when I went by there on Sunday. Before they left."

"Left?" Audrey asked for me, as I was too confused to even form the word.

"Oh dear. Those two parents of his, dammit, I just want to wring their necks," Aunt Debbie snarled between cigarette drags. "Have a seat. Can I get y'all a Diet Sprite or beer?"

We sat down on the cat-hair-covered sofa, which smelled like a pet store someone had just microwaved a Lean Cuisine in.

"I don't know how much you know about Christopher's past. What his mama and daddy have put him through." She took a seat on the massage chair she undoubtedly passed out in every night.

"The pray-the-gay-away camp?" I asked. "He told me about it."

Aunt Debbie nodded. "Right. All those counseling retreats. It's torture, if you ask me. They threw a fit after he brought you to the barbecue and since he was already grounded when y'all snuck out for 'ice cream,' they made it even worse when he was caught," she said.

"It was frozen yogurt," I corrected her.

She rolled her eyes, then winked. "Whatever you boys are calling it nowadays."

Clearly, Aunt Debbie had a very different idea of what Christopher and I had been up to, but I was in no mood to explain that *frozen yogurt* was not slang for gay sex.

"Anyway," she went on, "I don't know all the details, but after what happened at that dance, Jim and Angela pitched a fit. Christopher called me and tried to get me to come calm them down, but it was too late." She shook her head, staring sadly at the cloud of cigarette smoke floating in front of her.

"What do you mean 'too late'?" I asked.

"They sent him off to another one of those awful programs."

"You mean another pray-the-gay-away thing?" I could barely speak. I could feel my throat tightening in shock and rage and confusion.

"I don't know if they can legally call them that anymore, but yeah, one of those horrible counseling programs. I begged them to let him come stay with me while they cooled off, but once Jim and Angela get an idea there's no stopping them. And what with the new church they're starting out here and after what happened back in Missouri, in their batshit-crazy eyes, they've got too much to lose."

I couldn't believe what I was hearing. When you'd grown up the way I had, these types of homophobic extremists were like the bogeyman. You heard about them on TV or online, but you never really imagined them affecting your own life.

"What happened in Missouri?" Audrey asked.

"Jim's board of directors at the ministry found out about Christopher's being gay and all, and somebody told somebody who told somebody until the whole church had turned against them. They all but ran them out of town, which is why Jim decided to relocate his whole business and start fresh here. But if he's going to make this place a success, he can't have all that drama again. So he's nipping it in the bud before it can become a problem."

"Nipping it in the bud? By sending their son off to some brainwashing experiment?"

"I'm so sorry, sweetie," Debbie said, and I could tell she really meant it.

I didn't know what else to say. Or how to feel. Or what to do. So I just sat there staring at the envelope. Afraid to open it. Because then all of whatever the hell was happening would be real. I stayed on that sofa for a long time, until a cat peed on my shoe and we got out of there.


I kept the envelope on my lap the whole ride home. Was he breaking up with me? Or was it a passionate declaration of love?

At first Audrey remained quiet, eyes on the road. But finally she couldn't stand it any longer, and asked, "Are you going to read it?"

"I think I want to wait until I'm home," I told her.

She nodded.

I'd watched the world happen from a safe distance at my

little window for as long as I could remember, and now, suddenly, I'd been pulled into the drama of real life.

Neither my mom's Prius nor my father's Vespa were in the driveway when we pulled up, and I breathed a sigh of relief for some much-needed peace and quiet.

"Are you all right?" Audrey asked as I gathered my things from her backseat.

"Just confused," I told her.

"Me too," she said. "I mean, I knew his parents were a little nutty, but this is bizarre and intense."

I could only nod in agreement. I just wanted to go sit on my bed and read his letter. I kissed Audrey good-bye and thanked her for the ride and the company.

"Anytime, my darling," she purred. "Ring me if you need anything."

I went inside, not even stopping for a glass of water in the kitchen even though my mouth was completely dry with nerves. I rushed to my room, shut the door, and stretched out on the bed. I unfolded the piece of yellow legal paper with his scribbly handwriting on it and began to read.

*Dear Marley,*

*By the time you get this, I'll be at yet another counseling "retreat" run by my father's colleagues. Isn't that a hilarious word for a place that attempts to brainwash kids into not being gay? Retreat. Picture a spa but instead of* deck chairs and cucumber facials, it's twelve hours of Bible study and processed food.

I'm writing you this for two reasons. First and foremost, to tell you I'm sorry for what happened at the dance. I lost my temper. I was so happy that night, so excited that we'd pulled off getting to a school dance together, so relieved to have won in the ongoing game against my parents . . . that when that kid said those stupid things, I lost it.

I'm so sick of fighting, whether it's my parents and their friends or idiots at school or politicians in the news. I'm over it. And I guess I hit my breaking point. Like I said, I'm sorry I ruined what up until then had been a really special night.

The second reason I'm writing is a bit more complicated. I'm over it, Marley. I do a good enough job of pretending I'm not fazed, but I am so over fighting my parents to accept me for who I am. The reality is that I'm just going to have to keep fighting for the rest of my life or until I give up and they win. Up until I met you, I thought I might let that happen, but not anymore. I'm done. I'm going to run away and I wanted you to know about it because I don't want to lose contact with you. I'm going to *leave the camp Friday night—and I'm not coming back home.*

*I hope you're rolling your eyes at my dramatics because I certainly am, but I guess I just want to disappear from these people's lives for good, and running away feels like the only option. This isn't coming out of nowhere for me, as it's something I've thought of doing for a long time; I've just been too scared. All I've ever wanted in life is to make a difference so that kids going through the crap I've been through don't have to go through it anymore. I used to think I could fight but now all I want is to be free. I want to be happy and to live my life out in the open and not under some evangelical microscope of disapproval.*

*I am not sure where I will go. Maybe take a train to New York? Or a bus out west to California? What I'm asking from you is a ride to the bus or train station . . . and, most importantly, a chance to say good-bye.*

*So if you don't think I'm totally insane (or even if you do), meet me Friday night with your car, at the address below, at eleven p.m. That's late enough that everyone will be asleep and so I can sneak over the fence without getting caught. If you don't want to get wrapped up in* all of this, I completely understand. I just need to do something before it's too late. I'll watch for you and if you don't show up then I'll get the message.

Regardless, I just wanted to say thank you. I'd never known what it felt like for someone to care about me the way you've cared about me these past few weeks—and to care the same way in return. To connect with someone so easily. To have a friend. You've opened up the world for me. And for that, and so much more, I thank you.

Love,
Christopher
Hampton Campgrounds
1001 Cedar Mill Rd.
Greensboro, NC

# NOW

I'M FULLY AWARE THIS PLAN Christopher was proposing was fraught with potential disaster. Running away in the dark of night? Talk about dramatic. But the reality is that it happens more often than you'd like to think. So many gay teens are pushed to the breaking point, pushed further than a teenager should have to be pushed while also dealing with the fact that we're just kids with all the hormones and insanity that go along with that. We're teenagers, we make stupid decisions, but sometimes they're to save our lives from the people who are trying to destroy them.

If I could go back in time and start over, I'm not sure what I would have done. Maybe I wouldn't have let him try to run away but instead would have brought him to my parents until we figured out what to do. Maybe I would've called Audrey and asked for help. Maybe I would've taken him straight to the train station. Maybe I wouldn't have gone to pick him up at all. I don't know. I'll never know, because that's not how these things work. These things happen and our lives are never again the same.

# THURSDAY, SEPTEMBER 27, 8:01 p.m.

I HADN'T SAID MUCH FOR all of dinner. Neither had my parents, for that matter. Their financial optimism had wavered. We had reached the *just don't talk about it and maybe it'll go away* phase. Which had turned into *just don't talk at all.*

"The bok choy is very tender," my dad said to no one in particular.

No one agreed or disagreed; we just kept eating. The overall mood in the room was one of complete distraction: my parents with their obvious financial drama, and me thinking about Christopher's letter. Cedar Mill Road was an hour outside of town, out past the water tower. It was a campground every North Carolina–based Boy Scout or Girl Scout had peed outside at. I knew the way there . . . but it wasn't the getting there that I was worried about. I didn't want Christopher to run away and become homeless or be in danger of any kind, but I also didn't want him to stay stuck with his parents.

Most selfishly of all, I didn't want to have to say good-bye to him.

"The tofu is very tender," Dad added after a while, which made Mom let out an annoyed sigh and drop her fork onto her plate with a loud clatter. She got up, taking her plate to the kitchen, then went to bed.

Dad and I just sat there for a while. It was the first time I noticed all evening that there wasn't any music playing. It's always surprising how loud silence can be.

"No circles of enlightenment tonight, I guess?" I asked, a bit more chastising than I had meant to sound.

Dad let out a sad chuckle.

"You know, I am fully aware that we're ridiculous people, Marley," he said, peering at me from over his glasses.

"You're not ridiculous," I replied without much commitment to my defense.

"No, no. I am. When I met your mother, I didn't have a clue about any of the mumbo-jumbo spiritual stuff she was so devoted to. I was yet another gangly English major with an affinity for pretty, long-haired girls. And when I saw your mother, I said to myself, 'There's the woman I am going to marry.'" His face shimmered with the memory.

I wondered how far a person changes for love. Or if it's love that changes the person. Maybe a bit of both. My father's whole being had been shaped and molded by my mother. Not that he was some kind of puppet—he was as passionate and independent as he ever was—but the outlook on the world and his ways of dealing with it were all things he had learned from Mom. Who we are before love is different from who we are after.

Would I be the same after Christopher as I'd been before? Was I completely insane for wondering this about the first person I'd ever fallen for?

Dad went on. "And as we spent more and more time together, I guess you could say she rubbed off on me. Her magical way of looking at the world inspired me to see things a bit more colorfully, a bit more hopefully."

Color and hope. Christopher.

"But I'll be honest, Marley—I do sometimes wish we were a bit more practical about things. Maybe then we wouldn't be in this mess. But on that token, practicality doesn't inspire the way magical thinking does. Y'know?"

I knew what he meant. And I wondered whether it was practical or magical to help carry out Christopher's plan the following night. Perhaps a braver version of myself would've opened up in this moment, asked my father what to do, asked for help. But I didn't. I simply nodded and sat there until it was late enough for me to go to bed.

Once I got there, I lay down and stared at the ceiling, wondering what Christopher was doing at that exact moment. I wondered if he was staring at his own ceiling and thinking of me. Or thinking of his plan for the future. And I wondered if I had the strength to help him carry it out.

# FRIDAY, SEPTEMBER 28, 4:55 p.m.

SET CREW WITHOUT CHRISTOPHER WAS like a cruel joke of after-school punishment. The idea of "after-school activities" should mean *leaving* school, getting as far away from the place as possible and being free to do your own thing without the presence of your peers. Set crew was no such enterprise.

We had been using dish sponges to create the effect of leaves across one of the canvas flats for close to two hours, the entire time of which I'd spent playing out the scenario of going to pick up Christopher that night.

"DARLING!" a voice that was unmistakably Audrey's brayed behind me. "You missed a spot."

"It's a sponge. That's sorta the point," I said without turning around.

She grabbed my shoulder and physically turned my frame to face her.

"The independent movie theater is doing a ten o'clock showing of *Bram Stoker's Dracula*. We simply MUST go. I've never seen a Coppola on the big screen! Can you even imagine?"

Ten o'clock would *not* do. But I didn't know whether I could tell Audrey why.

"I don't think I can make it, babe. Sorry," I apologized.

"Why not?" Audrey immediately replied, giving me zero opportunity to make up a believable excuse.

"Because . . . I have stuff tonight."

"What kind of stuff? Eating ice cream and watching *The Real Housewives of* whichever one airs on Friday nights?" She sassed back at me like one of the Real Housewives themselves.

"First of all, there isn't a *Real Housewives* that airs on Fridays."

"Oh," she replied. "That must drive you nuts."

"Yes, in fact, it does. But tonight I have . . ." *Think fast*, I told myself. *She knows you too well.* "Plans with my parents."

She stared at me, her brooding, dark eyes reading my soul like a fortune-teller weighing whether or not you're the type of gullible person she can convince to buy her an expensive ruby in exchange for eternal happiness.

"Oh well. Next time, I guess." She sighed, which made me sigh. My sigh, however, was one of relief.

I couldn't believe I was doing it but I was doing it. I was driving down a long, dark road to pick up Christopher so that he could run away to his future. I was officially an accomplice in his escape to freedom. To be honest, the intensity of it all felt pretty cool. It was definitely the most badass thing I'd done in my entire life. (Which isn't saying much. Before this, the most badass thing would've probably been the time I stole two dollars to buy a Coke out of a jar in which my second-grade class was collecting money to send to some disaster-relief fund in a third-world country. Come to think of it, that doesn't really make me badass so much as a complete monster. But show me a seven-year-old who ISN'T a monster!)

The road out to the campground was completely dark and I was driving as carefully as possible, sure that at any minute a deer would jump out in front of my car.

As the gate to the campground loomed in the distance, the clock in my car read 10:59, but it was a few minutes fast. I slowed down even further and dimmed my headlights to avoid drawing attention. I pulled over to the side of the road and peered through the chain-link fence surrounding the place. Most of the cabins were dark, a few lit by the bluish glow of bug zappers. It was the perfect setting for a horror movie or, in this case, a homophobic brainwashing camp for teens.

I decided it'd be best to turn off the lights completely, as well as the motor. So I sat there in the stillness of my car. It was spooky but invigorating, knowing that at any moment Christopher would appear through the trees.

I glanced down at my phone a few times out of habit but was met with zero reception. My parents wouldn't be looking for me—I'd told them I was spending the night at Audrey's. Not even Christopher was sure I would be there, which meant no one knew where I was. This was an oddly exciting feeling. I was fairly certain it was a feeling I'd never experienced before and one I made a mental note that I'd like to experience again.

Absolute invisibility from the world as I knew it. I farted loudly just because I could with zero embarrassment, and immediately regretted it because it was too late to crack a window.

Just then I heard footsteps in the grass and crispy leaves, moving quickly. I leaned across the seats to stare out the passenger-side window and was startled by the sight of Christopher sprinting toward me.

I pushed open the car door like someone in the getaway car of a bank heist, and Christopher slipped in just as smoothly, slamming the door and shouting, "Drive!"

I fumbled for the keys, made a quick U-turn in the middle of the street, and floored it back down the dark road.

Christopher sat panting, out of breath, sweaty but smiling. Relief and elation radiated out of him in the darkness of the car. We were quiet—I didn't know what to say to someone who'd just escaped a propaganda therapy center and I figured it'd be best to let him speak when he was ready.

Finally, he squinted and looked around the car.

"What smells like ass in here?"

I quietly thanked God the car was dark enough for him not to see my face, which was one of utter humiliation.

"You farted, didn't you?" he added, then cackled a loud, relief-filled laugh. "What a lovely welcome gift."

"I was all by myself and I got carried away!" I shouted in defense. Then I gave up and joined him in the laughter.

"Well, for God's sake, roll down a window!" He felt around for the window button, eventually finding it; the cool air of the passing woods hit our faces with freshness.

"You came," he said after the laughter died down and the car aired out. "Thank you."

I wanted to look him directly in the eye and tell him of course and that I loved him and that I didn't want him to run away. But I didn't say any of that or look him in the eye because I was driving and also because I'm a coward.

"Are you okay?" I asked, unsure what else to say.

"I'm okay. I'm way more okay now than I was earlier. I'm now the okay-est I've ever been." He hung his head out the window like a basset hound and howled a cry of joy into the moonlight.

We kept driving and I sorted through the billion questions I had for him about the past week, about his parents, about the night of the dance. I didn't know where to start.

"Does anyone know you left?" I asked.

"Nope. Not yet. I left a note, so they'll find out tomorrow." His hair flapped in every direction, like an octopus flailing to electronic dance music.

"What did you say in the note?"

He took a deep breath, cleared his throat, then said as simply as you'd say you needed to go pee, "I told them I had killed myself."

My stomach dropped like it does on roller coasters that go upside down, and it took everything in me to keep from slamming on the brakes in shock. Instead I simply shouted, "What?!"

"Calm down. It's not like I actually *did*. I'm not a ghost, if that's what you're worried about," he reassured me. Then, playfully, he added, "*Or am I?*" He let out an evil laugh.

"Don't do that! Dammit. Why would you say such a thing?" I demanded.

"Because," he said, "it's the only way no one would try to find me. And because I wanted to make a point. These lunatics think they're fixing me or helping me or whatever, but they're not, and they need to be faced with the fact that their actions are far more damaging than helpful."

I didn't respond. I didn't know how to respond. I didn't know the protocol for discussing someone's fake suicide.

"Don't freak out," Christopher said, putting his hand on mine. "It's for the best."

"For the best? What are you even talking about?" I was pissed but I wasn't really sure why. Maybe it was the strangely visceral prospect of actually losing him.

He pulled his hand back, rested his arm. "Look. I need to get away from all of this. You know that. I thought that maybe a new town would calm my parents down, but it's not going to. It's only making them worse and it's only going to get worse. So what? Am I supposed to suffer through this BS until I grow up and move away? I don't think I can wait, Marley. I don't think I'd survive it."

This was some intense stuff for me, a guy who usually spent his Friday nights watching Bravo and eating ice cream.

"Where will you go?" I asked, after what felt like a two-hour moment of silence.

"Wait. Is that the water tower you took me to?" He was distracted, staring through the trees. "The Spot!"

"Yes. It's down that road," I said, annoyed, wanting to get back to what mattered.

"Let's go!" He clapped his hands with the excitement level of someone at a football game, not in a dark car after faking his own death.

"Now? Don't you think it's a weird time for that?"

"Why?" he replied without missing a beat, and I didn't have an answer. The truth was that this was a weird time for *anything*. We might as well go hang out at the water tower where teenagers went to make out.

With a shrug and a head full of even more questions than before, I pulled off onto Old Mill Road.

The place was empty. Most people visited The Spot in the earlier hours of the evening, before curfew. After I pulled the car up right beside the tower, Christopher jumped out and began to run around the parking lot.

"I don't have to live with my parents anymore!" he shouted loudly into the sky. "I'm dead!"

"Don't say that!" I shouted with actual rage, stomping onto the pavement and slamming my car door.

"I'm just being funny."

"It's not very funny."

Christopher rolled his eyes and wrapped his arms around my waist, pulling me into him. We rocked back and forth, like we were slow-dancing.

"*Sorry,*" he said with a mocking exasperation . . . but he was staring into my eyes, so I was too transfixed to put up a fight. "I'm not dead. See." He kissed me. "Can a dead person do that?" He kissed me again, this time a little longer. "Or that?" His hand moved under my shirt. His fingertips were cold, and I could feel my skin bristle into goose bumps at his touch.

"I've really, really missed you," I whispered into his neck.

"I've missed you too," he said, kissing mine.

"What are you going to do?"

Our voices were so hushed we might as well have been in a library. With each word, we seemed to get quieter, as if the words themselves were beginning to get in the way.

"I'm going to kiss you again." He placed his lips gently onto mine.

"I mean, about life; where are you going to go?" I asked from beneath his lips, spoken through our kiss.

"*We* are going to go lie down underneath that water tower." He took my hand—mine was clammy, his was warm and soft. "And you're going to stop talking."

He walked, pulling me behind him, over to the water tower. He stretched out onto the concrete slab beneath the tower, where generations upon generations of teenagers had shared moments like this one. The same place many had experienced their first true intimacy. And as I stretched out beside Christopher and he looked into my eyes, I knew I was about to have mine.

As we lay there together, as we touched and kissed and clutched, you could *feel* our joy. It was in the air, a cloud of satisfaction and euphoria.

"Can I ask you something?" I asked, which is always a ridiculous thing to say, because what is the person supposed to do? Say no?

"I think I know what you're asking, and yes, I *am* gay," he joked.

"Shut up," I told him. "Is this . . . I mean, how does it compare to being with other boys?" I felt more and more humiliated with every word that came out of my mouth, but what else was new?

"*That* is what you're thinking about right now?" He rolled over onto his side to face me. "For real?"

"I know that's stupid. It's just that this is . . . wow . . . like I don't even know what to do. I mean, it's really, really nice. But I have nothing to compare it to. And I'm worried I'm just . . . getting it wrong? Or maybe it's really, really nice for you too?"

"Are you asking if I'm enjoying myself? Are you not here? Is it not abundantly clear?"

"Okay, I know you're *enjoying* it . . . but I guess I feel you have more experience, and have gone further, and I just don't know how this compares to *that*," I said through a tightened mouth.

He sighed and sat up, looking down at me. The moon was fixed right behind his head like a halo or crown or hipster fedora.

"I've only gone all the way once, and it was different from this. Not bad but different. It was this kid at camp and we didn't really know each other that well. I think we were just so freaked out by the therapy that we wanted to see if the world would end if we had sex. So we did it, and it didn't."

I nodded as he slipped his shirt and jacket back on, the air getting chillier by the minute.

"Is that what you want to hear—that this was different?" he asked. "Because it was."

"You don't have to patronize me," I fired back before I could weigh the boldness of the statement in my head.

"I wasn't!" he shouted defensively.

*What the hell am I doing?* I wondered to myself. Here I had just had the most magical time with the most magical boy and now I was starting a fight over the way he'd answered an awkward question I'd asked.

"I'm sorry," I said. "You weren't patronizing, I'm just being weird. I'm just . . . this is incredible, and I guess I'm freaking out because I have no idea what I'm doing. I only know I want to do it."

As he stood up, he grinned at me, that same grin he'd given me at the supermarket the first night we spoke.

"This really *is* incredible," he said, looking down at me. "Do you hear that, world?" He spun around dramatically, shouting at the night sky. "This is incredible! Being with Marley is INCREDIBLE!"

"Shut up!" I said, laughing now.

"I'm sorry, I can't hear you right now. I'm too busy thinking about how incredible we are!" he called out, grabbing hold of the water tower's ladder and swinging himself onto it. "I'm sorry, Marley, but I need the world to know that you are, really and truly, unlike any boy I have ever been with before! Because this, world—THIS IS REAL!" He began climbing the ladder to the top of the water tower.

At this point, I was convulsing with laughter; he'd gone from scrawny gay teen to Marlon Brando in *A Streetcar Named Desire* within seconds.

He pounded on the empty tower as he ascended the ladder. Shouting "incredible!" and "Marley!" the whole way.

I pulled on my shirt and ran out to look at him atop the tower. He stood there, proud and beautiful. Just then he began to shout again, but he slipped—he slipped and began to slide, letting out a quick "Oh shit!"

Exactly how it happened is still hard to remember because I was so lost in the moment before. The moment I still dream of going back to. When I try to remember what comes after, it's like a collage. I can see his face, the stars, the moon, the tower, the ladder, my sneakers still on the ground, him falling. But none of it forms into a total picture. It's as if the moment itself was thrown to the ground and shattered into a million pieces.

I remember thinking it was part of the joke, part of the comical proclamation of his passion.

I remember laughing at first, as his foot tripped on the pipe.

I remember thinking how ridiculous and hilarious he was being, as his legs went out from under him on the slippery metal roof.

I remember the sound of his sneakers, making this high-pitched squeak as he slid to the tower's edge, like nails on a chalkboard.

I remember him saying "Oh shit" as his hand reached out behind him, grabbing on to nothing.

I remember him, in what seemed like no time at all, falling, crashing down.

I remember screaming.

I remember him falling.

I remember screaming.

I remember him hitting headfirst onto the pavement.

I remember this horrible foreign noise as his skull met the earth. Not quite a crunch and not quite a crack.

I remember screaming. Not for help—there was no help. Just screaming.

I remember running over to him.

I remember seeing him there, motionless, with his neck twisted sideways at an angle necks aren't supposed to twist.

I don't remember what I said to him.

I don't remember if I said anything at all.

I don't remember shouting for help.

I don't remember being able to help, because I couldn't.

I remember a sense of choking as a terrifying shock took over my entire body.

I remember the moment when I went from shock to the moment I knew he was dead.

# NOW

YOU GRIEVE AND YOU GRIEVE and you grieve, and at some point you wonder if the grief will ever run out, but you quickly realize that there is a limitless supply of grief. It is there when you reach for it. It is there when you don't reach for it. It can seep between the cracks of any wall you put up. It can invade even the happiest of thoughts. It can even hijack your dreams. Grief can find you no matter where you are, no matter how far you've traveled.

I'm in the backstage hallway, heading over to the greenroom to see what food they have tucked away in there. The food situation in my dressing room is less than ideal. I've been greeted at just about every one of these speaking engagements with the same unappealing platter of sliced veggies and hummus. I've had it up to here with hummus. I am thinking that: *I've had it up to here with hummus.* And then very quickly, I am thinking, *You have no right to complain about any of this. You have been living in an alternate world ever since Christopher died. This is not reality. Reality died at the water tower.* This is the progression of pretty much every thought I have.

Look at me, in this new, altered reality. I am the pretty (after hours of hair, makeup, and Instagram filters) gay boy whose boyfriend killed himself because of his homophobic preacher parents. I am the beautiful victim and the world loves me for it.

Or at least that's the story I'm selling.

Just a week before I came to New York to accept this award, Harrison called with even more "big news": I'd sold a book about my experience. A book that would be published as a memoir but was actually fiction. The book advance I was being offered would save the house my father's book-advance gamble had lost.

This is what my life has become. All because Christopher's life will never become anything other than what it was.

I didn't do any of this for money.

I did it because of what happened right after he died. I did it to prevent the real Christopher from becoming entirely erased.

I must remember that, but everyone around me is making it harder and harder to do so.


When I get to the greenroom, I am immediately greeted by Janice Atwood, the executive director of the LGBTQ Society of America, which exists to promote LGBTQ positivity, especially for those under parental disapproval and family scorn. Janice is a lovely woman who left her mega-important CEO job at some Silicon Valley start-up to devote her life to helping others. She's got these long blonde-and-black dreadlocks that hang down to her butt and she's maybe the coolest and calmest human being I've ever met. She has no idea she's backing a fraud.

"Hey, mister," she says the minute I walk through the door frame. She's filling a little paper plate with yogurt-covered pretzels.

"Hi," I say, nervous. Janice always puts me on edge. I guess it's because it's intimidating to be around someone who has devoted her life to good.

"Get this! The silent auction raised close to half a million dollars tonight!" she says in a voice that gets an octave higher on every word. "And we haven't even closed the bidding on some of the big prizes. You should feel proud to have been a large part of that, my friend."

"Yeah." This is the most I can come up with. I don't feel proud. I can't, even though I know in some small and moderately screwed-up way, I *have* helped.

"Hey . . . I know all of this has been a lot, buddy." She stares deeply into my eyes, the way only a truly good human being can. "But you better remember that Christopher is somewhere up there, and he's so damn proud of you."

"Thank you," I say, turning to leave the room.

I've officially lost my appetite.

# SATURDAY, SEPTEMBER 29, 1:15 a.m.

I RUSHED TO MY PHONE and dialed 9-1-1.

It did that thing where it said *DIALING* for what felt like forever because I only had two bars out by the tower. I began pacing, or at least I think that's what I was doing. I had never dialed 9-1-1; it's such an odd feeling. Seeing those three numbers on your own phone for the first time.

Finally, an operator answered.

"Nine-one-one, what's your emergency?"

"Someone has . . . My boyfriend . . . I think his neck is broken."

"Where are you?"

"I'm at the water tower, out on Old Mill Road. He was . . ."

She was already dispatching an ambulance before I could finish.

"Hurry. Please," I implored. Then I hung up. I don't know why I said to hurry; I'd felt his pulse as well as I could remember how from my health class freshman year. He didn't have one and he wasn't breathing and his heart wasn't beating and his neck wasn't even human.

*What do I do?* This was the only question repeating over and over in my head. *What the hell do I do? Who do I call? Do I call his parents? Do I call my parents? Do I call Audrey?*

I shook his stiffened body, screamed for him to wake up and talk to me. I'd never seen a dead body before. It's indescribable in its strangeness. So human, yet so hollow. I don't know if I believe in God and I don't know if I believe in spirits or ghosts or whatever . . . but something is missing when you look at a dead body. A person, with open eyes and an open mouth, but not quite a person. More like a painting, but there, right in front of you, in your arms.

"Wake up," I heard myself whisper as I cried some more. I don't know how long I waited there until the ambulance lit up the darkened silence with its flashing sirens. At some point the sounds, along with those of tires on the loose gravel, surrounded me. Paramedics came rushing over. I don't remember what happened next. The paramedics trying to revive him and putting a blanket over me as if that would somehow help anything whatsoever. Eventually cops arrived and taped off the area with crime-scene tape.

As they loaded Christopher's body into a body bag, I understood that, officially, he was gone. A numbness took over my entire body. I honestly think you could've put me in boiling water in that exact moment, and I wouldn't have felt it. I felt nothing, I saw nothing; I was asleep in a terrible nightmare, yet awake in the middle of the forest.

A robust, older policeman came over to me and asked if I felt all right enough to talk to him. Looking up at his kind face and the face of his colleague, a much younger woman with a black ponytail and friendly smile, I agreed.

"We received a police report over an hour ago that a Christopher Anderson was intending to commit suicide. Can you identify this body as his?"

A body. That's what he had become. Not a human, not a person; a body.

"Yes," I said, immediately remembering the suicide note. "But . . ."

I stopped myself. I don't know what it was, but something in my mind told me to stop myself.

"But what, young man?" the cop asked as I felt all the blood in my face go somewhere between feet and ankles.

Here was the moment I could have told the truth. I could have explained the story in its entirety, from his parents to the camp to the escape plan to our wonderful night. But I didn't. All I could do was think about him and every moment we'd had and how he'd told me, once upon a time, that what he wanted in life was to fix things for kids left in the position he'd grown up in. This current scenario was, admittedly, not exactly what he'd meant, but I wasn't thinking about that, or anything rational, for that matter.

"But . . . I tried to stop him and it was too late."

As the words left my mouth, I knew I'd done a very, very bad thing. I had lied about something so terrible that, if there did end up being a God, I would never be forgiven. I felt guilt from the top of my head down my spine to the bottom of my toes. But it didn't stop me from unleashing the story of his parents and the camp and the therapy and how horrible they'd been. I was vomiting up every word inside of me. I gave them every detail of his life as I knew it, leading up to this catastrophic mistake.

Except for one very, very important part.

# The North Carolina Journal

Police responded to a 9-1-1 call just after midnight Saturday morning reporting someone having fallen off the Old Mill Road Water Tower. Police and paramedics arrived at the scene and found the body of an unconscious teenage male, age 17. The young man had broken his neck and died instantly in the fall. The body was later identified as Christopher Hank Anderson, son of Reverend James and Angela Anderson. The Andersons, known for their televangelism empire, had only recently relocated to North Carolina. There has been no word on whether the death was accidental, intentional, or foul play. Funeral arrangements are being made for Wednesday morning.

# WEDNESDAY, OCTOBER 3, 10:15 a.m.

THE REST OF THAT NIGHT was a blur that lasted until the sun began to come up Saturday morning and a new day began and life continued on with frustrating similarity. I'd never lost someone I was that close to, aside from grandparents, but something about losing a grandparent felt expected and normal. Losing someone who not only happens to be your age but also the person you had fallen in love with—that's a whole other kind of despair.

The way life goes on after death is infuriating. You want to shout at the newscaster giving the weather updates about clear skies for the rest of the week that they should show some respect and not wear a yellow tie at a time like this. You want the whole world to feel what you feel. Which is especially maddening when you're not entirely sure *what* you feel. For me it was hodgepodge of shock, devastation, anger, and overwhelming guilt.

Mom and Dad had shown up at the water tower the night of the accident as soon as the police called them. So had Christopher's parents.

This was not how I'd imagined them meeting.

In fact, I'd never imagined them meeting. I'd always thought of me and Christopher as . . . apart.

My mother seemed more overcome with emotion than Christopher's, who maintained her steely expression and clenched lips as she and her husband identified the body and spoke with the police and comforted each other.

They did not talk to me. They did not ask me anything. They did not want to know their son's last words.

Already, I felt myself being erased from their version of Christopher's life. I might as well have been an anonymous hiker who'd found him lying there. I might as well have been no one to them.

Mom and Dad drove me home in silence. Once or twice they asked if I was okay, and then we all just sat there, reflecting on what a stupid question it was. I was not okay. I was pretty sure I would never be okay again.

When we got home, Mom asked if I wanted to talk and I said no and they told me that they would give me space but that they were there when or if I wanted them. Sunday and Monday and Tuesday, Mom cooked all my favorite foods and even let me order pizza WITH a gluten crust. Audrey came by every day, but I wasn't in a place to talk to her. I just wanted to be alone, to grieve in peace and to figure out what the hell was true and what wasn't. It was true that he hadn't killed himself. But it was also true that if his parents hadn't sent him away, hadn't punished him so harshly, he'd still be alive. I didn't want to let them off the hook. I wanted them to feel the hook as painfully as I was feeling the hook, and I didn't care how screwed up that might have seemed.

Christopher's parents had planned a funeral for Wednesday morning at eleven a.m. Mom bought me some black pants and dress shoes to wear and left them outside my door. I could hear them getting ready in a strange silence that seemed to fill the house. Whatever tension had existed between my parents had been lifted in the wake of the tragedy. That's one good thing about horrible deaths—they *do* put stuff in perspective.

As I attempted to figure out how to tie my tie in the mirror, I looked at the reflection of myself for the first time in days. The dark circles under my eyes gave the pupils a gray, depressing hue. My hair was a crime scene and my skin was paler than a vampire's. My mouth was the weirdest part of all, my lips appearing to be stuck in a downward position that was not quite a frown but something worse; it was expressionless, like a painting where the artist got too tired to finish the mouth and gave up.

I looked awful. But I felt worse.

Dad knocked on my door.

"Come in," I said. It was odd to hear my voice; it was like I hadn't said a word in days.

Dad came into my room, dressed in the same old suit he wore for really happy or really sad occasions.

"Need help with that tie?" He was already tying it, well aware of my lack of coordination when it came to accessories, or pretty much anything for that matter.

"Thanks," I managed.

"How're you holding up?" he asked as he straightened the now tied plaid tie.

I shrugged and he nodded. Then we just stood there for a while, staring at the little flecks of color on the off-white carpet.

"I can't understand why a kid would do that. He was just a boy," Dad said, unable to help himself, and I could tell he regretted saying it immediately. "Sorry."

"It's okay," I said, and took his hand, feeling a rush of guilt so heavy that I almost told him the truth. Mom appeared in the doorway, in the kind of black cotton dress you only wear to funerals.

"We should get moving," she said.

How could I explain to her that I was incapable of moving? How could I explain to her that it felt like time had stopped?

I couldn't.

So I went to the funeral.


Throughout the ten-minute drive to the church, Mom and Dad went to great lengths to make small talk about whatever they could come up with. Making half-finished statements about houses we passed or unenthused observations on the lack of rain as of late. Mom blamed it on something having to do with the upcoming harvest moon. It was as if they'd been challenged to do whatever it took to keep the car from being silent.

Outside the church, people were already filing in. Two news vans were stationed on the curb, eagerly broadcasting the story of the conservative preacher's gay son who committed suicide. Audrey's was the first face I saw in the crowd, and she threw her arms around me. She was crying.

"I'm so sorry, darling," she said.

I squeezed her tight and wondered if I should pull her into the bathroom right then and there to explain everything. Maybe then this paralyzing guilt would weaken and I could breathe.

"There are Christopher's parents. We should pay our respects," Dad said, walking over to them.

"We don't really know them," I said, uncomfortable.

"We should pay our respects," he repeated. *Because we were there*, he didn't add.

I had no choice but to follow him over.

"Jim, Angela . . . we're so sorry," he said. They looked up at him, then Mom, then me with a look of growing horror. "I don't know what to say, except that you've been in our thoughts and prayers all week."

Christopher's mother looked to his father, as his father looked around at the people nearby with one of his forced million-dollar smiles, and then eventually toward the news vans. He cleared his throat, staring down at his shoes.

"May I speak with you privately?" Christopher's father asked my father. Dad followed the reverend a few feet away. It was unclear what they were discussing as I stared from where I was standing. I looked to Christopher's mom but she was already turned away and walking into the church.

"What's going on?" I asked.

"It's all right, love," Mom said, putting her arm around me. "Audrey, how about you go inside and find us some seats?"

Audrey nodded and disappeared into the aggressively quiet sanctuary. Soon after, Dad returned to us, his expression pale and confused.

"What was that about?" Mom asked.

Dad shook his head in disbelief and said, "He asked us to leave."

"Leave where?" Mom asked.

But I knew. Dad's next words were a punch in the gut, but they weren't a surprise.

"Here. The funeral."

"What?" Mom raised her voice, then looked around, embarrassed.

People were passing us, headed inside. The crowd had thinned out. Who were these people? Did these people even know Christopher?

"Let's just get in the car," Dad said; his face was becoming less pale. In fact, it was becoming red with rage and humiliation.

"I don't understand," Mom said.

"Those assholes," I muttered under my breath. "Those complete and total assholes."

Dad took my hand. "It's all right. Calm down."

"I don't understand what's happening," Mom repeated, over and over, as we walked across the parking lot toward the car.

"I do," I said, my voice rising. "And they can't do that. I was with him. I was his boyfriend. I loved him. I . . ."

The church doors shut and I heard an organ begin to play some depressingly monotone hymn. Dad was staring at the news cameras, which had been focused on us for who knew how long.

"Let's just get in the car," he said, turning his confused face away from the gaze of the cameras.

I didn't get to say good-bye to him. I didn't get to be there as he was carried from the church and laid into the ground. I didn't get to hear the things that were said about him—even if they were lies, even if it was incomplete, I didn't get to hear his name said over and over and over again. I didn't get to be there in the middle of everyone else's grief. Audrey, who had never really hung out with Christopher, got to be there. But I didn't get to be there. It might have been easier if they'd done it to punish me. At least punishing me would mean recognizing that I played a role in their son's life, but no.

Instead, they opted to make me disappear.

"What in the world is wrong with those people?" Mom wondered aloud as we walked through our front door. She hadn't stopped talking since we'd left the church and I hadn't tried to stop her because then I would've had to speak and I didn't know what I'd say. "I know they're hyper-religious, but the audacity to tell us to leave a funeral? I am dumbfounded!"

Dad was already taking off his jacket and tie, tossing them onto the back of the sofa.

"You hear about these kind of people on TV, but you never think you'll actually run into them," Dad said. "We've met our fair share of conservative Christians, but this is something else altogether. How many of these camps or retreats or whatever they call it did they put that boy through?"

"Is it even legal for them to forbid us from entering a funeral?" Mom paced back and forth, barefoot now, her heels kicked off into a corner.

"What kind of interaction have you had with these people?" Dad sat down on the sofa, looking at me.

"Very little. I met them at his aunt's party and then again the other night at the water tower," I told them.

It was an odd feeling to be so hated by two people I'd barely ever spoken to. My phone was lighting up with a string of texts from Audrey asking where we'd gone. I started to imagine the funeral that was taking place a few miles away. I thought of the casket containing Christopher's body. I wondered if it had been open or closed, if they'd covered him with makeup and putty to hide the bruises and scars from the fall. If they'd tried to make him seem as lifelike as you can make a dead body seem. What was being said about him? What was the story his parents were making sure he left behind?

"I need some tea." Mom headed off into the kitchen, a ball of nerves.

"Dammit," Dad said after a while. I'd only heard him curse maybe five or six times ever. Usually when attempting to install electronics. "I don't understand people sometimes. Humans can be such monsters." He took a breath, closing his eyes for a moment, and opened them again as he exhaled, calmer. "I'm so sorry you're going through this, buddy. Losing someone is unexplainable enough, but the hatred these people are showing . . . it's unimaginable. I don't know what to say. I wish I did."

He didn't need to say anything. All I wanted in that moment was to go back to my room and be alone all over again. If I hadn't lied, I wondered, would I have been able to walk into that church? This, however, was a pointless question, because the answer was clearly no. Christopher's parents wanted nothing to do with me and they wanted me written out of his story no matter what.

I texted Audrey and explained what had happened. She was just as furious as the rest of us and went on to tell me all about how Christopher's dad got up and gave a eulogy where the blatant focus was debunking the rumors that his gay son had committed suicide because of his family's disapproval. In fact, he went on to explain that Christopher wasn't even gay but psychologically imbalanced and that his suicide was something they had feared would happen for a long time.

And just like that . . . Reverend Jim Anderson and his wife, Angela, got their wish. They got to remember their son as the person they always wanted him to be instead of the person he really was. They fixed their problem. They got to show the world that they were, despite tragedy, as perfect a family as they seemed on TV. My strained and albeit insane attempt to make Christopher's death mean something had been in vain. The story's ending had been rewritten by yet another lie, as Christopher's parents sat in a church with all their friends, fans, and followers and pretended to understand.

# SUNDAY, OCTOBER 7, 5:45 p.m.

I COULDN'T BEAR THE THOUGHT of going to school. My parents told me I could take the rest of the week off, to "acclimate."

But there's no way to acclimate to a hurricane. You just have to suffer through it, and even then it's unclear how things will ever settle down again.

I stayed at home. Or not even that. I was home, sure. But really, I stayed in my own head. I refused to leave it, despite how claustrophobic it was beginning to feel. I replayed every moment I'd had with Christopher, and was traumatized when I realized I was already forgetting some of them. His voice—what did his voice sound like? I didn't even have a voice mail to remember him by. Just texts—texts that I read and reread. Then I moved on to the letters, to his handwriting. I was devastated by every sentence, every letter, even every emoji. And the whole time, I was also ridiculing myself, calling myself all sorts of awful things, telling myself I had no right to Christopher, since I'd only known him for a little less than a month, as if time has the power to dictate one's heart. But grief didn't care about any of that. Grief didn't care about months or minutes. Grief had its own measure of importance, its own measure of time.

There had been witnesses. I knew people at school would be talking. They would know what we were. They would know that we'd been together. His parents couldn't erase that. Kids would talk and, despite normally hating gossip, a part of me took comfort in the fact that at least Christopher would be kept alive in the hushed lunchroom conversations of my peers.

And I was right—the kids at school *did* talk. I knew this because that Sunday evening, the day before I was supposed to return to school, our doorbell rang. I heard it from my room and didn't think much of it. I'd been in bed all day long, which, if it weren't for the soul-crushing sadness and guilt I was experiencing, would've been my idea of a lovely day.

Ten or so minutes after the bell, Mom tapped on my bedroom door.

"Marley?" she said in the kind of soft voice you'd use around a sleeping baby. "There's someone here who wants to speak with you."

"Ugh. I told Audrey I needed to be alone," I said without sitting up from my mattress, which had become a graveyard of dirty dishes and crumbs.

"It isn't Audrey."

"Then who is it?" I asked with a little too much sass for the occasion.

"His name is Harrison Holbrook and he says he's here to help you."

The ridiculousness of the name Harrison Holbrook aside, how could anyone help me at this time? Unless of course he was somehow going to bring Christopher back to life.

"Just put on some pants and come out here for a second," she said, gently shutting the door behind her.

It was the first time all day I'd noticed I wasn't wearing pants. I begrudgingly threw on the cargos that lay crumpled by the bed. They smelled like stale peanut sauce and body odor. I headed into the living room.

Mom and Dad were quietly talking with a man who was sitting on the sofa. When I walked in he immediately stood up and faced me. He had a handsome face that was heavily manicured and wore a fitted, expensive-looking suit.

"Harrison Holbrook." He projected as if onstage, thrusting his hand toward me. "Holbrook PR."

I shook his hand and couldn't help but notice his fingernails were the cleanest I'd ever seen.

"Hi," I said, looking at my parents to find out what the hell was going on.

"Harrison just arrived from New York and has a lot to talk to you—well, all of us—about. Are you good on tea?"

Harrison patted his mug with a contented smile. "All good, Sharon."

Mom smiled back at him.

I had no idea what was going on.

Harrison leaned in. "Marley, I run a public relations firm that handles highly sensitive yet politically important cases and stories. Your situation was brought to my attention by a colleague who is reporting on the death of Christopher Anderson. You were his boyfriend, correct?"

I was frozen with suspicion but nodded nonetheless.

"And you were with him when he committed suicide?"

Those words had yet to settle into the fabric of my mind. They still conjured something deeply upsetting inside of me every time I heard them.

"I was," I lied, staring down at Harrison's very polished shoes.

Harrison glanced at my parents, then back at me, then back at my parents. Then he let out a pronounced sigh.

"All right, here's the deal. We all know that Christopher's parents are two of the most homophobic people on television. They've built an empire on despising people like you and me. I know people who witnessed you and your parents being barred from his funeral and I know what was said in the reverend's eulogy. Have you seen their statement to the press?"

I shook my head.

"Here, let me read it to you. 'It is with great sadness we announce the death of our only son, Christopher, who took his own life last weekend due to his severe mental health issues. Christopher had been at a counseling facility in the week leading up to his death. Despite great efforts from talented therapists and pastors, he resisted progress and eventually ran away from the facility with the intention of taking his own life.' My sources also tell me that they're saying to people that Christopher's body was found by a stranger."

*A stranger.* Just when I didn't think I could hurt more, I did.

Harrison shook his head. "Their statement to the press is nothing but an attempt to bury their son's story deeper than the casket he's currently in." He stopped, contemplating his words, then added, "What I'm saying is that they've decided this story ends with the burial of their son and the continuation of their homophobic beliefs and efforts to harm our community, from their endorsements of gay brainwashing therapy to their support of every antigay bill we've seen passed in the last decade. Now their son is dead, a suicide. And from what I hear, this was after a week in one of those pray-the-gay-away treatment places. Funny how they don't mention that, isn't it? Tell me, Marley—did you love Christopher?"

"I did," I whispered into my lap.

"I can tell you did. Marley, a horrible and terrible and frighteningly inexcusable thing has happened. But with this tragedy comes an opportunity. A chance to right years' and years' worth of the wrongs his parents have caused our nation, our people, their son."

I could still feel the softness of Christopher's lips on top of mine. I could still smell his face as I kissed his cheek.

"Despite tragedy, you've been given a chance to help kids like Christopher. You've been given a responsibility to help fix things, once and for all. And if you'd like to pursue this kind of change, I would love to help you do it."

The room and everything in it seemed to spin around me. I understood exactly what he was saying. He wanted to take down the hypocrisy of Reverend Jim and he wanted to use me to do it. And despite a nagging feeling in my gut, I agreed to follow along.

For Christopher, I told myself.

Everything would be for Christopher.

I was not going to let his side of the story die with him. No matter what it would take.

# NOW

HARRISON BOUNDS INTO MY DRESSING room. I can smell that he's been heavily partaking in the open bar at the party below us. Fancy gay events have seemingly endless open bars, and it has yet to become clear to me whether the fancy people attending said events are there for the cause or the free vodka.

"I just bumped into Robert Watson from *Gay Lives* magazine. I don't know what he's been pumping into his face, but it's not making him look any younger." Harrison blows through his insults like the breeze through a wind chime, easily and with clatter. "I *think* I might have just secured you a cover story in two months!"

His smile is inescapable, so I force one of my own.

"That's nice," I lie.

"*Nice?* Are you kidding me? It's fantastic! Last month they had that lesbian chef who invented zero-calorie chocolate, and before that those triplets who came out on *Ellen*!" Harrison plants a big, wet, boozy kiss across my forehead. "Baby's first cover shoot! Mazel tov!"

At some point, this all stopped being about Christopher's death.

"It's bigger than that," people keep telling me. "It's bigger than one person. It's bigger than one suicide."

But here's the thing: It doesn't feel bigger.

Christopher's death will always be, to me, the biggest thing of all.

I know what I'm doing might help other people.

But it's not helping me. And I worry it never will.

# TUESDAY, OCTOBER 9, 11:35 a.m.

IT HAD BEEN JUST OVER a week. The world had existed with one less person for that little time. I still hadn't been back to school—I wasn't ready, and, with Harrison around, there were suddenly other things to do. Audrey came by the house after school on Monday with some assignments for me, but I couldn't really talk to her about anything other than homework— the first time she and I had ever done *that*. I had a hard time pretending around her; she knew me too well. A true best friend is like a walking diary you've scribbled all your hopes and fears into. The issue, however, is that when you don't want to face these hopes and fears, you don't want to face your diary.

I could tell she suspected something was up, but she never would've asked because it was also possible that I was just upset. Asking someone who just watched his boyfriend commit suicide what was *really* happening was just not something she could do.

Tuesday morning was tightly run by Harrison, who had set up camp in our guest room as if that wasn't weird at all. My parents too seemed unfazed by this. Everyone appeared to be far too focused on getting my side of the story heard to notice that our lives had been turned upside down.

I was seated on our sofa, wearing a wireless microphone running underneath a starched button-up shirt Harrison had given to me from his own suitcase that morning.

Harrison's assistant, Alex, a perfectly agreeable twentysomething girl with layers upon layers of makeup covering more acne than any adult should be physically capable of having, was testing the camera attached to Harrison's laptop. Alex had arrived in town on Monday afternoon and everything had moved incredibly fast since then.

"His skin looks green. Can we get him a different shirt? Red isn't his color. And are those our only lights?" Harrison rattled off, eyeing two enormous lights on tripods, looming over our sofa like vultures.

"I've got two more in the van," Alex said, heading outside.

"Do you need us to do anything?" Mom asked, timid and a little frightened in her own home.

"Is that what you're wearing?" Harrison asked, squinting at the sundress my mom had chosen.

"Yes?" she said.

"Let's go for something a little more mainstream, down the middle, crossing the party aisle kind of look. Know what I mean? We want all-American mom, not Stevie Nicks on Earth Day." Harrison turned his attention to Dad, who wore a plain gray sweater. "And how about you put a collar underneath that sweater and comb your hair? Otherwise you guys are perfect!"

Harrison smiled, the kind of smile I would later learn was as phony as his highlights. Mom and Dad nodded, agreeably yet visibly out of their comfort zone as they went to their room to change. I felt a pang of guilt, a tug in my gut, the kind of tug I would later learn was a whisper from the universe telling me to turn back. But, as I did a lot in those few months, I ignored it.

Alex lugged the additional lights into the room, knocking a framed photo of Mom and Dad's wedding off the wall in the process. Neither she nor Harrison seemed to notice, or at least they didn't care. We were doing a Facebook Live "press conference"—which, needless to say, would be the first time I'd done anything like that.

"We've got ten minutes, people. Ten minutes!" Harrison tapped his Apple Watch as he checked the camera's monitor with the new lighting. "Looking good. We've *got* to change his shirt, though."

Before he could even finish his sentence, Alex was unbuttoning the red shirt and pulling it off my body, switching it out with one that was identical except for its blue fabric. Mom and Dad came back out, Mom now in plain navy pants and a white button-up shirt. Dad had added a dress shirt underneath the sweater and taken off his glasses. They gave a needy look toward Harrison, like two lost children hoping for a father's approval.

"Fabulous! Perfection!" he shouted at them, clapping his hands. "Sit down right here, on either side of Marley." He placed them on the sofa, physically shifting their bodies into the angle he wanted. They were both sweaty from the bright lights and nerves.

"Alex, maybe one less light—now it's *too* bright," he said. Alex clicked off one of the movie lights. Finally, Harrison let out a satisfied breath of air. "Just perfect. All right, now, can you read this, Marley?"

He tapped a key on his laptop, lighting up the teleprompter he'd set up. We'd practiced this well past midnight the night before, as if I were studying for a spelling bee.

"Yes, I can."

"Okay . . . everyone ready? Here we go."

He pressed a button on the camera, a red light turned on, as he pointed at me, mouthing, *Go*.

I closed my eyes. Thought of Christopher. Not of him falling. Not of him on the ground. But Christopher smiling. Christopher, banished to a camp dedicated to undoing his identity. Christopher, not allowed by his parents to be who he needed to be. *I'm doing a good thing*, I told myself, but I wasn't sure I believed it.

I opened my eyes. And I began.

"Hi. My name is Marley McNally, and these are my parents, Sharon and Greg. I am making this video because last Friday night my boyfriend, Christopher Anderson, took his own life." The first six times we'd rehearsed, I hadn't been able to get past this line, the words seemingly lodged in my throat. Now I took a deep breath and kept going. For him. "Christopher was the son of Reverend Jim and Angela Anderson, who you might know from TV. They've made big careers out of denouncing gay Americans in the name of God—including their own son. Their son, my boyfriend, was gay, and they hated this so much that they forced him into treatment facilities using the 'pray-the-gay-away' method from the time that he was thirteen up until he ran away from one here in North Carolina last week. They don't want this part of Christopher's story told. They don't want the world to know that they had a gay son because they think it would ruin everything they stand for. But the truth is that while preaching this kind of hate, they were also direct-ing it at their own son. And this went on until their son couldn't take it anymore." *Christopher*, I thought. *What the hell am I doing?* "I only knew Christopher for a short time. We met and fell for each other really quickly, maybe too quickly, but that's what people my age do. I can't sit by and let his parents rewrite who he was. That's why I'm making this video. So that the world knows the real Christopher Anderson. A sweet, funny, loving, silly, and beautiful gay teenager who fought really hard to be himself."

On this last part, I lost it. I felt the tightening, then the tears, then the shame for shedding the tears on camera.

I'm not sure if I was crying just for the loss of Christopher or for, in this precise moment, the loss of myself in the midst of everything that was happening.

# TUESDAY, OCTOBER 23, 3:39 p.m.

WITH THAT ONE VIDEO, SHIT hit the fan and my insignificant world exploded, just as Harrison had planned.

The first person to pick up the story was some political gay blog I hadn't heard of. Then another one, and another one, followed by someone with a verified Twitter check by their name. By the following Sunday, the story had made it to CNN, the *New York Times*, the *Today* show. People made reaction videos to it on YouTube. A Facebook page Harrison set up to remember Christopher had hundreds of thousands of likes in its first days. I was officially *gaymous*.

Harrison was flying higher than a kite about the attention the story was getting, but kept insisting that he wanted it to be a *famous* story, not just a gaymous one.

"We're still weighing offers, and we wouldn't even consider it without something in writing, Gail." Harrison spoke into his phone now, almost shouting, while he paced around the living room.

Ever since the video went viral, newspapers and TV shows had been calling our house trying to get an interview. It was the first time I'd been grateful for Harrison's presence in our home, because neither my parents nor I had *any* idea what we were doing. Apparently, the first interview would be integral to how we unfolded the whole story.

I had been back to school, and it was surreal, like Christopher was the one who'd died, but I'd become the ghost. People told me how sorry they were, but they didn't talk to me much longer after that. A few cheered to me that they'd seen my video—as if I was a celebrity, not a mourner. Like this was a story line on everyone's favorite TV show and not my own depressing life. Audrey tried to protect me, but that was hard, because the biggest threat came from within. I couldn't tell her that. I couldn't tell her anything, really. And a part of me wanted her to call me on it—I almost resented that she was letting me get away with my silence.

Mostly she expressed her support for me by saying unprintable things about Christopher's parents, who had basically responded to my video by saying I was a liar, and hadn't known their son at all. Which only made me more certain that doing what I was doing was the right thing to do.

If Christopher could no longer speak for himself, I had to speak on his behalf. Simple as that.

When Harrison finished his call, he slammed his phone down triumphantly.

"BAM! We got *The Evening Report*!" he shouted. "A featured fifteen-minute interview segment!" He danced around the chair my dad liked to read in, pumping his fists in the air. "Boom! Boom! Bam!"

*The Evening Report* was the biggest syndicated nightly news show on television. It covered every topic from the crisis in the Middle East to why Jennifer Lawrence couldn't eat turkey ("the reason might surprise you!").

"That's good, right?" Mom asked. Through my whole life, Mom had never watched TV for, as she put it, "political reasons." These reasons were never explained nor discussed nor, for that matter, asked about. I was always happy for the additional space on our DVR.

"Good? It's one of the biggest outlets on television for this kind of story!" Harrison said so excitedly, he was almost singing. "This is huge. They'll be here Thursday morning!"

"*Here?*" Dad asked. "Meaning they'll be shooting in our house?"

"Yes! It makes the whole thing far more human!" Harrison said, too busy typing a text to notice the irony of attempting to make death more "human."


Late that night I texted Audrey. I felt too guilty to sit in silence watching *Say Yes to the Dress*, which was exactly what I was doing. (Has anyone ever said NO to the dress?)

I wrote: **Hey**.

She wrote: **Hey**.

Our generation and its endless contribution to vocabulary.

**Sorry I've been MIA**, I wrote.

**I get it**, she replied quicker than seemed possible.

**Where are you?**

**In bed, idiot.**

It was almost midnight. I really was an idiot.

**Wanna meet me by those swings near your house?** I wrote, aware that it was a moderately ridiculous request in the middle of the night. The swings in question were in her neighborhood park, a mere ten minutes from my house. It used to be the kind of park kids had birthday parties in by day and that junkies shot up in by night, but ever since the installation of security cameras, it was more just the former.

After an annoying forty seconds she wrote back, **Ugh. I'm not even wearing lashes but fine. See you in fifteen.**


I beat her to the park, which wasn't a surprise. I sat down on a swing and pushed off. *Push and pull.* That's what my dad used to say when he taught me how to swing. *Push your legs out, then pull them in.*

Finally, well over half an hour after the decided time, Audrey arrived.

"Sorry I'm late, doll," she said. I appreciated her predictability.

She kissed me on both cheeks, undoubtedly leaving enormous red lipstick marks on both sides of my face. I both couldn't and fully could believe that she was wearing a fresh coat of bright red lipstick in the middle of the night. She dropped down on the swing beside me and pushed off. Then pulled.

"Why is that the way we all learn to swing?" I asked, soaring through the air. "Push and pull."

"No clue. But it's a nice metaphor, isn't it?"

"How so?" I asked.

"Life is kind of like that. You have to push it and then pull it back."

"Calm down," I said at her uncharacteristic sincerity, and she cackled into the night like a witch.

I couldn't remember the last time I'd been on these swings. Maybe someone's birthday party? Maybe just a random afternoon after school with Audrey before we both hit puberty and turned into such terrible weirdos who resented everything that once brought us joy.

"So, you're having quite a week," Audrey said, after a long bout of silence accompanied by the rustling of squirrels and who knew what else in a bush behind us.

"Ha! That's one way to put it," I replied.

We kept swinging for a bit. Push. Pull.

"Are you okay?" she asked. I had hoped she would ask this very question . . . but I didn't have an answer. I guess part of me wanted to confess everything to her, to unload the guilt I was carrying.

"I guess so," I said, a coward pushing down the truth I so desperately needed to share.

"Yeah?"

"Yeah."

The rusty chains of the swings sounded like they were whining back and forth to each other.

"What're you going to do?"

"About what?

"All of this. That video you did. It's going viral. People at school won't shut up about it—and we're talking about some of the most cluelessly out-of-touch people in the history of humanity."

"I don't know *what* to do," I said freely into the night air. Something I hadn't been able to do this entire time of dealing with Harrison.

"What do you mean?" Audrey asked.

I had a lifetime's worth of telling Audrey everything. The first time I had a sex dream, the first time I watched *All About Eve*, the first time I said I was gay out loud, the fact that I didn't think Ryan Gosling was that hot, the reality that the cast recording of *Hamilton* went completely over my head. I had confessed everything to my best friend and here I was, biting my tongue.

"I don't know," I faked. And I could tell that in the back of her mind she knew I was pretending.

"What do you mean that you don't know what to do?" she pried.

This was my chance to unveil the truth to someone, a person who would understand. And I wanted to. I want you to understand that I really wanted to. But I wasn't sure what would happen. Not to me but to Christopher's story. I wanted people to continue talking about it, him, all of this. And maybe that was a selfish desire. Maybe my need to have the world talking about him was so that he wouldn't go away just yet. He could live on a little longer in the news articles, the flashes of his picture on the nightly news, and the whispered conversations of others. If I couldn't see or speak to or touch Christopher ever again, maybe I could at least live in a world where everyone else mourned him as much as I did, and maybe that would make the numbing pain that I felt all over my body subside, even for just a second. And, most important, maybe if enough people said his name out loud, then he would never disappear at all.

"I just don't know," I said.

"All right. Well, I understand where you're coming from, darling. Just know that you've got someone on your team. And it's me. You can tell me anything. Deal?"

This statement alone made me feel calmer. I locked my hand around hers as we swung in the nighttime silence. We kept swinging. Pushing and pulling. As if we'd never grown up.

"What's this for?" she asked, her eyes motioning to her hand.

"I don't know. Just you, I guess," I said. And I meant it. Maybe later it would be considered deceitful, but in this exact moment, I really, really meant it.

# THURSDAY, OCTOBER 25, 11:00 a.m.

"TELL ME ABOUT WHEN YOU and Christopher met," said Liz, the reporter from *The Evening Report*. For emphasis, she held a pen up to her chin, the signature body language for a reporter who wants to indicate to the audience that this is a serious interview.

We were seated in two chairs across from each other. Three cameras loomed down on us. The pressure on me was so palpable it was almost comical.

"I saw him first at school. The first day of school, actually," I said. "But we didn't talk until we ran into each other at Shoppers Plus."

"Aw. Don't you just love Shoppers Plus?" the reporter asked with a bubbly demeanor of someone interviewing a talking cat.

"Um. Yeah. Sure," I said.

"What's your favorite thing to buy at Shoppers Plus?" she continued with an eager grin. I looked to my parents, who shrugged.

"I buy batteries sometimes. And groceries." This was the

best I could muster, and it seemed good enough for Liz, who leaned back in her chair, nodding enthusiastically.

"And was it love at first sight?" she asked. I winced at the absurdly clichéd phrase. "For Christopher, I mean, not Shoppers Plus. We *all* love Shoppers Plus!"

*Christopher would find this funny*, I told myself. *If Christopher saw this, he would be laughing.*

"I really liked him, if that's what you mean," I said with a nervous laugh.

I locked eyes with Harrison, who was nodding along with every question and answer, like a proud parent watching his child's piano recital.

"I've been told that Reverend Jim and Angela Anderson forbade you from entering Christopher's funeral. Is that correct?" Liz asked, her voice firmer and more direct.

"Well, *forbade* seems like a strong word," I said, catching sight of Harrison furiously shaking his head out of the corner of my eye. I backpedaled. "It was my dad they spoke to, but they basically said that they didn't want us there. So, yeah, I guess they did."

Harrison gave me a thumbs-up.

"If you could say anything to Christopher's parents now, what would you say?" Liz asked. You could hear how proud she was of her question from just her tone of voice.

I had so much I wanted to say to them. Some of it too explicit for national television. Most of it, actually.

"I guess I'd just say that they had a really special son. And I was lucky enough to get to know him for a few weeks. And I'm so sorry they lost him. But I wish they'd honor who he was and not try to reinvent him for their own sake. The world is full of gay kids just as wonderful as their son, a lot of them going through the same disapproval from their families that he went through. And it's bullshit." I slipped, hearing the bleep in my head that they'd be sure to add in. "Sorry. I guess what I'm saying is, I hope that if his death can mean anything, it's to remind parents to unconditionally love."

Liz smiled at me without appearing to have heard a word I even said.

"Well, that's great. Let's hope something can come out of this tragedy. Here's Kyle Rogers with a report on gay suicide in the United States."

The interview was over—the monitor cut to a prerecorded segment about kids all across the country who'd been like Christopher: denied their identity, forced to change . . . or at least forced to try to change. I could hear their stories as I took the mic off and handed it back to the technician. I could see their faces on the monitors as Liz thanked us and the producers pushed release forms into our faces. Each kid's story was unique, but they also had so much in common. Their fates could have shifted so easily, if the people they loved had been kind to them. Yes, their ends were different, in truth, from Christopher's. But that seemed like a small detail.

"You did well," Harrison said as we headed to the kitchen (aka the greenroom).

"*And* you did good," Dad added.

I really hoped he was right.

# SATURDAY, OCTOBER 27 and SUNDAY, OCTOBER 28

AFTER THE INTERVIEW AIRED ON *The Evening Report* the following night, it felt like everyone in America was talking about the story. Reporters and news vans were parked outside our house all weekend, attempting to get a comment from me or my parents. Harrison handled them like the pro he was.

"We appreciate your interest in the story, but the McNally family is not conducting any further interviews at this time. This is private property and we ask that you remove yourselves from the premises," Harrison announced from the steps of our front porch to flashing cameras and aggressively shouted questions like he was the president of the United States announcing a ban on Reese's Peanut Butter Cups.

By the end of the weekend, I had a Twitter account, a Facebook fan page, an Instagram, a Snapchat, and all the other apps people use to document their lives and causes. Life had turned into one of the reality shows I loved to watch. The only difference was that watching a reality show and living one are nothing alike. For one, you can't pause life, go get a bowl of cereal, take a leak, then pick up where you left off. Also, a reality show isn't real, whereas actual reality is really, really uncomfortably real.

# MONDAY, OCTOBER 29

THE HIGH SCHOOL CROWDS I had invisibly navigated my entire teenage existence all seemed to notice me now. Every single person staring, whispering, pointing. Was this what being popular was like?

This bizarre feeling lasted the whole day. Teachers treated me carefully and delicately. Lunch ladies smiled at me. A really pretty popular girl even said hi to me. This was a whole new world . . . and I was beginning to think I preferred being invisible. Toward the end of the day, Audrey came rushing up to me in the hallway.

"There you are!" she said, out of breath from running in heels. "Have you seen it?"

"Seen what?"

She looked like she might be sick. "Oh, no. You haven't. It's everywhere," she said, shaking her head, her dangling earrings jingling with her every move. She pulled out her phone and the video was already paused on the screen. The image was of Reverend Jim and Angela sitting across from Liz! My Liz! *The Evening Report* Liz!

"Is that Liz?!" I gasped. Audrey nodded with dread and tapped play on the video. The interview began.

"Look, Liz, we knew our son. We loved our son. And he wasn't a homosexual," Reverend Jim said through his perfected fake smile that was both cheerful and respectful of tragedy all at once. He was really good at being on camera.

"If this is true, with all due respect, why would this young man continue to insist that he was Christopher's boyfriend?" Liz asked, pen to chin.

Christopher's parents looked at each other with forced sad smirks, shaking their heads at the craziness of the world, their scripted answers loaded and ready.

Christopher's father said, "What you're seeing is someone who barely knew our son trying to use his death to get famous. It's shameful but not surprising in this day and age. All we know is that our son wasn't a homosexual. He was a good, sweet, all-American boy. And suggesting anything otherwise is just plain incorrect."

"But what do you say to the sources who indicate the therapy retreat your son had been on the week prior was in fact gay conversion therapy? A practice you have publicly supported on numerous occasions?" Liz asked.

But the Andersons didn't even budge. They were cool, calm, and collected under this kind of pressure. They'd made careers out of it.

"It was a retreat for many things. Our son was there because he was mentally unstable. And we will not discuss that any further," Reverend Jim stated flatly.

"Well, I appreciate your sitting down with me. Next up: Olympians who shoplift, only on *The Evening Report* . . ."

Liz kept going, but I hit stop on the video. Audrey looked up at me with wide, disbelieving eyes.

"It's everywhere. All the blogs are on your side, though. Or at least the ones I read," she reassured me. "But, like, Marley, this isn't going anywhere. It's, like . . . on."

Audrey was right. It was, indeed, "on." However, I was decidedly off. I had this awful vision that Christopher was going to be forgotten, and all that would remain would be the fight over whether or not he was gay.

I knew he wouldn't want that part of him to be ignored or changed. But I doubted it was all he'd want to be remembered for. The fact that sexuality is *still* a way to describe a person will never cease to leave me shaking my head in confusion.

When I got home I went to the guest room to talk to Harrison.

He was packing up to return to New York, where he'd continue running my "campaign" (just what I was campaigning to become was still unclear).

"Come in," he said, the sounds of NPR playing low from inside the room.

He had all of his clothes laid across his bed, neatly folded and organized to an almost sociopathic degree.

"Hi, Marley. Did you get my email? This is all a really big deal! Congratulations!" he said, jumping with excitement.

"Which email?" I asked, feet firmly on the ground, with zero intention of jumping or being excited.

Speaking to someone like Harrison was tough because there was so rarely an opportune moment of silence. He spoke as if running through a long-winded agenda.

"The award! Oh God! You haven't found out yet. I get to see your face when I deliver the news. Okay, are you ready? You're being given the Hero Award by the LGBTQ Society of America!" He squealed like a little girl or adult gay man meeting Harry Styles.

"I am?" I asked, his words successfully avoiding the act of sinking in, more so just bobbing on the water like a fishing lure.

"Yes! They're covering the flight to New York, plus they're putting you up at The Hudson; they do the awards in the ballroom there." Harrison rattled off the details like a game show host telling you about the brand-new car and state-of-the-art refrigerator a person has just won for successfully coming up with the answer to some stupid trivia question like "Who discovered beets?"

"That *is* neat," I said, which was true. It was just, y'know, completely and totally undeserved.

"VERY neat!" he corrected.

"Okay, Harrison. I need to tell you about something," I said, staring at my shoes and wondering, for just a moment, how shoelaces get so disgusting-looking so quickly.

"Of course," he said while rolling a T-shirt like a croissant. "Is it about that *Teen Vogue* article? Because if so, I agree they should've used a better photo. I don't even know where they got that one. You look like a twink version of Ruth Bader Ginsburg.

No offense, of course—it was just the lighting. We'll never let it happen again!"

"No. It's about everything, actually."

He looked up at me, attempting to shield a startled expression. "All right. Of course. Have a seat," he said.

I took a seat on the old trunk in the corner of the room, the one Mom kept the Christmas decorations and summer solstice lanterns in.

"I don't think I can do this anymore," I said with a clenched throat.

Harrison sucked some air through his teeth, his mouth stuck in an emotionless poker face.

"And why is that, Marley?"

This almost made me laugh, both out of nerves and the absurdity of just how big a *why* we were dealing with.

"I'm going to confess something to you, but you cannot tell my parents and you cannot freak out and you cannot get angry and . . ."

He waved his hand, the universal sign for *shut up and get on with it*. I felt like Taylor Swift having to admit she had never actually written any of her own songs or someone else changing the course of human history.

"My story wasn't entirely true," I said after a breath so deep I felt it in my kneecaps.

Harrison slowly nodded, removing his glasses, cleaning them with his shirt, then putting them back on.

"All right. What parts?"

"He was my boyfriend. His parents did send him to those conversion therapy places, but . . ." I cleared my throat even though I didn't need to. "He didn't kill himself."

The color drained out of Harrison's face and the room was eerily still for what felt like a lifetime. He stood up from the end of the bed and began to pace around the room.

"Are you *sure?*" he asked, with a vague twang of desperation in his voice that told me I could keep the lie going if I wanted and he'd be more than okay with it.

"I am sure. He didn't jump—he fell. He was being stupid and trying to make me laugh and he fell. He slipped and fell. Just like that," I said with a snap of my fingers. The snap seemed to linger in the air.

"But he ran away from that week in the therapy retreat, after everything they'd put him through. He said he wanted to end the suffering." Harrison rattled off the story with urgency.

"But he was just going to run—he wasn't going to die. He wanted to get away from them," I said, the deep weight of guilt oozing through my stomach. "I wasn't thinking when I told the police what happened. I just said it and then all of this happened and it felt like we were doing something good, so I—"

"We *are* doing something good," Harrison interrupted. "We are doing something very, very good. The amount of awareness, the conversations we've started, we're making a difference. YOU are. Look at this award, for instance!"

"But based on a lie. How is that something good?" I said, with a boldness I didn't know I was capable of.

Harrison was uncharacteristically without a retort. Instead he sat back down on the end of the bed, closing his eyes and slamming a balled fist onto a pile of socks.

"All right—story time. I grew up in Utah. Did you know that?" he asked without looking at me.

"I didn't," I replied.

"Mormon. Big family, all boys. I was the youngest. And the only gay one. You can guess the rest of this story," Harrison said with a bemused sadness. "That conversion therapy crap, those camps, counseling with men telling me all about the fiery inferno of my future unless I changed my ways. And I tried. I tried really hard to practice everything they taught me to do, to ignore all the feelings they told me to ignore, to push it down so much that eventually it was bound to simply disappear somewhere in my stomach. A dangerous little flaw to avoid and deny with all the power in my soul."

"And could you? Avoid it, I mean?" I asked.

This made him laugh, which was a surprising response.

"I did. Or at least I told myself I was doing so for a while. And want to know the stupidest part of this whole thing? When I was managing to do so, or at least pretending to, it was the first time in my entire life my mom told me she was proud of me." He shook his head at the words he'd just said and let out a broken chuckle. "Look, I hope you never have to meet her— she's *such* a horrible mother. Terrible bangs too."

We both laughed for a second, unable to conjure up something more appropriate. Then it got quiet again, just the hum of a silent house.

"I thought I might . . . y'know . . . pull the big one, off myself, do the unthinkable before I hit my eighteenth birthday. But I didn't. And I still don't know why. I held on, who knows how, and then one day I got the balls to do it: I ran. I got on a bus to LA and I never went back."

I was lost in thinking about how many kids my age had been through the exact feeling Harrison was describing. Or how many were going through it as I sat there on a trunk filled with handmade Christmas tree ornaments and Chinese lanterns, in our guest room, with the opportunity to help change things. The opportunity I was trying to throw away.

"I'm sorry. I did a very, very bad thing. And I don't know why I did it," I said, as if that would fix anything.

"Bad and good are sometimes murky. Some things *are* very, very bad. Some things are very, very good. But most things are somewhere in the middle, in this gray area of intention," Harrison said, cracking his knuckles so loud I thought he'd broken them. "You went about this in a bad way, perhaps, but if your intention is good, if it's to try and change things, then you can't beat yourself up. You just have to keep going."

I understood his point but I also understood my own. The reality was that I had done some good while also doing some bad. But perhaps the truth would've resulted in just bad. Maybe by lying, I'd turned a bad thing into a good thing. This was, at the very least, the closest thing to an excuse I could find.

"Do what you want to do, Marley," Harrison said, looking at me not like a kid, but like a peer. "But remember, you're doing something. You're acting. We are fighting. And that, my friend, is a very, very good thing." As he said this, he looked like someone who had fought for too long to give up now, the face of someone who'd done it, who'd overcome, like Christopher escaping that night. And I wanted to help him. All the versions of him that were out there, that were being born that very minute. I wanted to fight. I had to.

After Harrison returned to New York, where he and his colleagues fielded requests for everything from interviews to endorsement deals to an offer to have me guest judge a cake-baking competition show, life slowly became somewhat normal again. Who knew tragic deaths could bring so much opportunity? I mean, besides pretty much everyone who has ever written a memoir.

I'd traded in my after-school activity of painting sets for speaking on the phone with reporters about suicide prevention pretty much every afternoon. There were magazine articles, photo shoots, more TV interviews, endless blogs. The attention was becoming less bizarre to me, and I'd successfully started to convince myself that this was a good thing. I'd started to find joy in the fact that I had found a purpose in life, to serve others. If I tried really, really hard, I could almost convince myself I wasn't doing anything wrong whatsoever.

After Harrison released the one and only photo of Christopher and me together (the one Audrey had taken at the dance), Christopher's parents stopped giving interviews and pretty much stopped talking about their son altogether. This was also likely due to the new book Reverend Jim had coming out just in time for Christmas, titled *Hands Off My Jesus*. I didn't read it, but judging from the cover image (a group of faceless men in suits attempting to remove baby Jesus from a nativity), it's safe to say it was about Reverend Jim's second-favorite topic next to abolishing homosexuality: defending Christmas.

Mom and Dad were back to forbidding me from eating gluten or processed food. With Harrison out of the house, they even started chanting again. I was back at school full-time. A brand-new *Real Housewives* had started, and the cast was reliably insane and fascinating to watch.

Life moved on . . . for most of us.

# FRIDAY, NOVEMBER 30

AFTER CHRISTOPHER DIED, EVERYONE AROUND me told me that "time heals everything," but as the weeks went by, I couldn't help but realize these well-intended words of wisdom were actually complete and total bullshit. If anything, time rubs salt in the wound as the world goes back to normal and you're left still in pieces.

My life, for all intents and purposes, *was* back to the normal routine, but I was not the same person I was before. I was someone else, someone I didn't even know, going through the motions of the person I was on the outside and hoping that by doing so I'd forget just how broken I was on the inside.

I wanted to talk about Christopher. Not about the tragedy or my pain or how grief can be so unpredictable or any of the other BS topics my school counselor, Mrs. Geary, tried so hard to get me to focus on. Mrs. Geary, a nice older woman who looked as if she'd been counseling students at the school since the Stone Age, had only the most positive intentions. However, they were also the most infuriating. She didn't know Christopher, had never even met him, so attempting to talk to her about him was about as helpful as the five bowls of cereal I'd taken to binge-eating every night before bed.

It was in the midst of one of those late-night, one-man food-fests that I found myself going down the wormhole of googling Christopher. The one good thing about his father being such a famous bigot was that there were lots of photos of his family. Just getting to stare at photos of Christopher and see his name printed throughout endless articles about both his family and his death was a very small but necessary comfort. Everyone on the Internet seemed to have an opinion about Christopher, his family, and in many cases even me. I couldn't help but feel a weird sense of pride for getting Christopher's story out there, the bulk of which was true, except for the big twist at the end. But it was creating a conversation, regardless of what did and didn't happen. People were discussing something very, very important: acceptance.

It was through this nosedive into Internet commentary that I found myself on Angela Anderson's personal website and blog. It was nothing like the flashy web empire of Reverend Jim Anderson, with its online store and video gospels and message boards. Angela's website sold no products and included very little except a photo of her family and a blog. The most recent post surprised me.

*I would like to start this out by thanking the countless friends and kind strangers who have reached out to offer their sympathy, support, and unique personal experiences with*

*tragedy. It is impossible to put into words
what a mother feels when losing her child, so I
won't attempt to do so now. The tragedy my
family has endured has changed me as a
mother, as a Christian, and as a woman. I loved
my son very, very much. Despite many reports
to the contrary, I loved my son unconditionally.
And I always will. This type of grief is
confusing, to say the least, and I hope that
if anything comes from this nightmare
experience, it will be a clearer understanding
of how to help those going through it in
the future.*

*Sincerely, Angela Anderson*

Something about her words and the rawness of her honesty told me she understood the full story more than she'd let on in interviews. Or perhaps, more than Reverend Jim had allowed her to do. *Unconditionally.* It broke my already shattered heart to think of Christopher's mom being stuck in the position of hiding who her son was while also grieving for his loss. Perhaps I had been awake too long, perhaps it was my desperation, or perhaps I'd eaten far too much cereal, but it was as if I was suddenly seeing Angela Anderson in a different light. Before I could let myself think it through, I clicked the contact tab on the website and began to write her an email.

*I know I'm probably the last person you want to hear from right now, but I just wanted to say that I'm thinking about you. And I'm sorry for what you're going through. Marley*

A more coherent person would have hit delete but I didn't because I was not a coherent person. I was a grief-stricken teenager. Perhaps I was reading too much into it, but it did seem as if Christopher's mom was attempting to say she loved her gay son . . . or, at least, that was the story I was pinning to my every emotion as I sat there staring at the family photo on her website.

Sometime late in the night I drifted off to sleep with my open laptop beside me and every light in my bedroom still on. I had a dream about Christopher. Not even an interesting one where we went somewhere cool or did something exciting; it was just an average day. We saw each other at school, we ate lunch together, we met up in the evening and went to T.J. Maxx and tried on discount jeans. Nothing monumental happened at any point, but even so, the dream still felt important. I could feel the warmth of his hand in mine. I could smell his breath. I could hear his laugh and watch his eyes glancing over at me when he didn't think I was noticing. It was just a typical day in a typical life and it was the greatest dream I'd ever had.

I awoke the next morning to the obnoxious beep of my alarm clock. I smacked the snooze button, nearly knocking over the open laptop in the process. As I tossed it to the other side of the bed, I noticed I had an email in my inbox.

The sender?

*Angela Anderson.*

My stomach tightened so much I almost had abs as I imme-diately clicked open. I was still in that surreal in-between place your mind tends to hover in after you've just woken up from an intense dream, so a part of me wasn't even sure I was reading correctly as I opened the message and began.

> *Thank you for your kindness, Marley. I know you're going through a lot as well. I wish I had words of wisdom but I do not. I wish this whole thing hadn't turned so dramatic but such is life, I guess. I hope that doesn't come across as flippant as I fear it does. All the grief books I read say that remembering this is a part of life and is the only way to get through it but I'm not so sure how anyone can ever fully believe that. Know that I loved my son—no matter what you might believe, I really did. And I can't speak for my husband, but as the weeks have gone by, I can't help but feel an overwhelming sense of appreciation for whatever joy you brought to Christopher's life.*
>
> *Best wishes. Angela*

It was the most words she'd ever offered me, in person or writing, and I didn't know what to do with them.

I reread the message a few times to make sure it wasn't an automatic response. I couldn't believe she would write me back, and with such humility as well. Was she acknowledging that she believed me? Was she acknowledging the error of her ways? Was she realizing that all of this could have been stopped with unconditional love? I couldn't answer any of these things. And I was already late for school.

The school day was as boring as the one before. The month-long change of pace had long since disintegrated back into the monotony of reality. People still looked at me differently; I was still the guy with the dead boyfriend who had been on the news, but a sense of normalcy had even developed around that. That had become my high school label: The Tragedy Kid. And while it wouldn't have been my first choice, it was strangely and pathetically comforting to have a personal descriptive among my peers.

The email from Christopher's mom didn't leave my mind for a second. I kept rereading it on my phone and searching for hidden meanings buried within the words. Was she openly acknowledging who Christopher was? Did Reverend Jim feel the same? Did she actually understand how much I loved Christopher? And what would I do with this new piece of the puzzle? I knew that Harrison would have the email circulating to every possible media outlet by lunch, the perfectly damning evidence that everything Reverend Jim and Angela had said in the past few weeks was a total sham. And perhaps Harrison had rubbed off on me a bit, because as I sat in the back of American History class I imagined that exact scenario playing out. For just those few moments I sat and allowed myself to hate Christopher's parents with all the fury that I'd been pushing down since that night when everything had happened. I allowed myself to despise their very beings and allowed myself to take pleasure in imagining their demise.

"Marley?" Mr. Lester called out to me across the classroom, snapping me out of my spiraling daydream.

"Sorry. What?" I asked, attempting to sound as much like someone who had been paying attention as possible. Everyone in class was staring at me, awaiting the answer to a question I hadn't heard being asked.

"Marley, let's try keeping our eyes open and our minds alert during class. Okay?"

I nodded, stared down at my textbook, and pretended to listen for the rest of the class.

# SATURDAY, DECEMBER 1

THE NEXT EVENING WAS OPENING night of *Into the Woods*. The show's running time was just under four hours but felt like at least seven. Audrey had done everything she could to steal every scene she appeared in, which made her come across as either a psychopath or promising character actress. I'm not entirely sure where the distinct line of difference lies.

"Darling!" she bellowed from across the stage, running over to embrace me and take the flowers I'd brought for her. "You came!"

"Of course I did," I said. She knew just as well as I did that if I hadn't come she would've tracked me down and murdered me, but I let her pretend to be surprised because that's what friends do.

"I really felt like I captured the inner human of Cinderella's Stepmother. Don't you?" she asked, baiting me to launch into a solid three-minute monologue of praise, which she stood savoring every word of.

"Can I ask you for a favor?" I said after she'd thanked me for my kind words like I was a random fan on the street. "Would you want to sleep over tonight? I really want to have a night like the old days, and by old days I mean three months ago, before all of this happened. I guess I just need to feel normal for one night. Does that make sense?"

Audrey smiled coyly.

"I'm just honored to be your form of normal."

I laughed for the first time in I couldn't remember how long, and it felt good.


Mom and Dad never cared if Audrey slept over because she'd done so since we were old enough for sleepovers. Usually our sleepovers consisted of watching a movie and eating whatever food we had in the house until we passed out. This evening was no exception. The movie was *Valley of the Dolls*, which we'd both watched a million times together and separately but it still always managed to deliver. If you've never seen it, it's basically about a great actress falling apart and taking a lot of drugs in the sixties. Minus the sixties and the great actress part, it's sort of like a biopic on Lindsay Lohan.

It was the perfect evening. No one was treading carefully around me like I was made out of highly emotional and breakable porcelain, no one was whispering about how impressed they were at my bravery, and I was just another kid at another sleepover watching a movie with his best friend. It was surprising to see just much I'd missed the boringness of my life. I had considered showing Audrey the email exchange with Christopher's mom but decided that tonight would be just for comfort.

We were onto our third bowl of frozen grapes and our

second bag of the candy Audrey had stolen from backstage. In other words, we were in a perfectly lucid food coma.

"I'm getting water," I said, standing up for the first time since we'd started the movie. My foot was asleep and my stomach felt like it had been hit by a bus full of snacks. "Want some?"

"Yes, please!" Audrey said, her mouth full of M&M's.

Mom and Dad had been asleep since we got home and the house was quiet. It was nice not to have Harrison and Alex working all night from the kitchen table. It was nice to walk into our kitchen and feel like life was almost like it had been before all of this happened. It was nice to just be filling a pitcher with water and taking two glasses back to my room.

Audrey was sitting up on the bed reading something when I came in. And the second I realized what it was, I almost dropped the pitcher.

"Audrey," I said, as if I were stopping her from walking into traffic.

"Marley. What is going on?" she asked with quiet dread. "This is the letter Christopher's aunt gave you that day we went to her house, isn't it?"

I had kept the letter under a book on my nightstand since the day I'd gotten it so that I could look at it before bed: his handwriting, his words meant just for me, a part of him I was keeping alive.

"You need to tell me what's actually going on right now," Audrey demanded.

I was caught, and what's odd was that I had this immense

sense of relief. Like a fugitive on the run who reaches the edge of a cliff with the cops behind him.

"Okay," I began, and told her the entire story. From the letter she was holding to the night I picked him up to us going to the water tower to the you-know-what to the fall and how I'd handled it in the moments after. I kept going through everything, all the way to my emailing with Christopher's mom the night before. The words poured out of me. It was the first time I'd said the entire story out loud, and with each word I felt a little lighter. The weight of this secret getting lighter and lighter. She sat there listening with a blank face, and I dreaded getting to the end of the story and having to hear her response.

"And it's wrong. I lied. I am a liar who somehow became a hero, but I didn't mean for it to go like that. I just wanted to teach his parents a lesson, and make his death mean something. Or else he was just another dead kid whose story no one would ever know."

"I see," she finally said after just sitting there staring down at Christopher's letter for a while.

"I'm a terrible person, aren't I?" I asked. I was already pretty sure I knew the answer.

Audrey had been by my side through many terrible mistakes and bad decisions. The time I cheated on my calculus final sophomore year. The time I stole a bottle of Coke Zero from a gas station just to see if I could. The time I lied to my parents and skipped school just to go watch the last *Hunger Games* movie in the theater three times in a row. But those were normal mistakes and lies; these were not claiming someone committed suicide.

"You have to tell the truth, Marley," Audrey said carefully, all her characteristic pizzazz disappearing from sight. "Then you have to apologize."

"But if I tell the truth and apologize, I make his father look right," I cried. "Christopher will be reinvented into their version of the story and no one will know how special he was. What if I send the email from his mom to Harrison—he can get it out there and show the world that Christopher's parents are lying, that they knew he was gay, and then they won't be able to erase how hard he fought for their acceptance. He won't just disappear and never come back—"

"He's dead, Marley. He's not coming back," she snapped, silencing me. "You can't reinvent your version of the story either. He's dead and, yes, his parents were awful to him, and, no, they shouldn't have put him through all those conversion treatments, but he didn't kill himself." Audrey was calm and rational, a genuine first for her. And she was making a good point that I so desperately didn't want to hear.

"But he wanted to make a difference. He wanted to fight for kids going through what he went through," I choked through tears streaming down my face. My words sounded more like an apology to the universe than anything else. "And now he is. Right?"

I hoped so badly to be correct but I knew in my heart I was not.

Audrey took my hand.

"We have to fight fair, Marley. Or what's the point in fighting at all?"

# NOW

AUDREY AND I DECIDED THE best way to deal with this would be to come clean at the awards ceremony of the LGBTQ Society of America. It would be the one place I could actually explain what I'd done in full and uninterrupted. My parents had decided to drive up to New York, so Audrey could tag along. The whole ride there had existed in that same awkward silence that has shrouded us in the days since Christopher's death. The trip almost felt like a second funeral, but one I'd be allowed to attend. But it wasn't clear whose funeral it was: Christopher's or mine.

So here I am, at the spot in our story where then merges with now. The moment we've all been waiting for, ready to fix my very, very bad thing.

"Darling," Audrey says, coming into my dressing room. "Isn't this an amusing turning of the tables?"

She means the dressing room. It's endearing to watch her attempt to act unimpressed by the showbiz excitement of it all. She's militant in her attitude that we're here to clean up my mess.

"Are you feeling ready?"

I shrug. "As ready as I can be, I guess."

There's a knock on the door before Harrison comes in.

"The stage manager just told me this is the five-minute warning. How're you feeling?" he asks. I feel bad for Harrison, since I'm about to ruin everything he's built around me. Hopefully the bigger picture—all those other teens for whom suicide was *not* a lie—won't be ruined too. Because that truth is much, much bigger than me. Or Christopher. Or anyone else.

"I'm feeling ready to get it over with."

I consider breaking the news to Harrison about what I'm going to say out there. I haven't told my parents either. (They're safely situated in the audience, at a table with Lisa Ling, Ariana Grande's gay brother, and Megyn Kelly.) But seeing Harrison's big proud smile, knowing what he's been through, knowing how his fixing of this situation is more about the fixing of his own past . . . I can't do it. I can't tell him. Yet another cowardly move in this story of a coward.

"Let's get you out there."

The walk to the stage is dark, narrow, and intimidating. I can feel the pulse of the hundreds of people awaiting me. I can hear the emcee, a drag queen from *RuPaul's Drag Race*, introducing me. I can feel the audience adjusting their bodies and minds in their seats to listen to something heartbreaking and moving. I can feel the tone of the evening changing all around me. The expectation of something meaningful to make everyone feel good about themselves. I can feel my gut tightening with the realization that this is really and truly about to happen.

They call my name, and as I walk across the stage, people applaud. The drag queen gives me as big a hug as her enormous gown would allow.

Then I step up to the podium.

"Good evening," I say into the microphone, one of those skinny bendable ones that looks like a black snake wearing a tiny winter hat. "Thank you so much for tonight's award."

I pick up the silver plaque, meant for an office wall of accomplishments. It's sweaty and glistening in my hand, catching the pink stage lights above me and mirroring them into my eyes. As I blink the blindness away, the audience is dead silent. They simply sit, waiting for the victim to regale them with his strength. I direct my attention back to the teleprompter screens on either side of me. I scan the words scripted for me to say next: *The past three months have been such a roller coaster.* I silently fume with resentment at this ridiculous saying—the past three months have *not* been a roller coaster, because a roller coaster is an amusement park ride that has a beginning, middle, and end, and only lasts for about two minutes. Everyone knows that. The phrase is meant to softly describe the ever-changing insanity of life but only serves to highlight its discomfort and frequent agony.

"The past three months have been such a . . . whirlwind." This is the first thing I come up with, and it feels right. I continue to read the words broadcast on the prompter. "But in the midst of all that, the support of the LGBTQ community has been an endlessly powerful inspiration and comfort. As most of you know, I am accepting this award tonight after the loss of my boyfriend, Christopher Anderson." The next phrase scrolls up on the screen: *who killed himself due to the isolation he felt from his homophobic parents.* But my throat tightens. I look to my right, into the wings, and see Audrey standing by the stage manager's podium, all her attention focused on me, her eyes holding me up, pushing me forward, and willing me to do the right thing. I look to the other side of the stage and see Harrison, his arms crossed and face stern with concentration.

"I need to tell you the truth. Because I haven't yet," I say quickly, afraid that if I slow down, I might chicken out.

I hear an audible gasp from the wings, Harrison's panic reverberating off him all the way to me onstage. I can feel it but I keep going.

"This award says the word *hero* on it and I can't stand here, holding it, pretending that I deserve it, because I don't. Christopher did. With all he went through and put up with from his parents, he *was* a hero. But I am not."

I glance over to Harrison, who is looking a little less panicked and more relieved.

"The truth is way more complicated than I or Christopher's parents or anyone has been able to explain. Because after what happened that night, everyone had a different version of the story they wanted to tell. People wanted to latch on to the story and use it and discuss it and analyze it until they could come up with the moral of this terribly tragic story. But sometimes the moral of a story isn't cut-and-dried."

I can feel the Facebook comments and the tweets beginning, every stranger on the Internet who felt a stake in my life as of a few weeks ago asking what the hell is going on.

"Christopher didn't kill himself. He wrote a suicide note, but his intention wasn't to die—it was to run away." I nervously bite a piece of chapped skin off my bottom lip; it stings and feels kind of good all at once. "Here's what's true: Christopher's parents *did* send him to conversion therapy retreats and pray-the-gay-away camps. Christopher's parents *did* know that their son was gay and wanted, more than anything perhaps, to fix this before people could catch on. They also knew about me. I was not some 'random obsessed kid from school,' as Reverend Jim tried to have people believe. I was Christopher's boyfriend, even if for just a short time. And I loved him."

The cast of *Wicked* has gathered together in the wings to watch my speech; it's a dreamlike sensation to feel the glittery green shadow of Oz's most talented citizens watching as I give a speech that could potentially destroy my life.

"Christopher asked me to pick him up outside the last conversion therapy retreat his parents sent him to and take him to the train station so he could run away," I go on. "And I agreed. Because, despite how overdramatic it all seemed, I had seen what his parents were putting him through and I knew that it wasn't going to get better. Christopher and I once talked about how the idea of the 'It Gets Better' campaign didn't work unless you *made* it better. If you took control of the 'get' part. Which is actually what he decided to do. I picked him up that night and we went to the water tower in my hometown for one last good-bye. And something stupid happened, and he fell off that water tower. He didn't jump. He slipped and fell and ended his life the night it had finally begun."

I look up at the projected image of Christopher's face above me, his beautifully crooked smile and freckled skin in the sunlight. A perfect-looking day at a lake. I wanted to ask him what lake and what had made him look so happy, but I couldn't.

"When the medics and the cops showed up, and the suicide note had been found, and everything was happening all at once, I just went along with it. Then, when his parents wouldn't acknowledge me or who he actually was, when they tried to rewrite who their son actually was, I guess I snapped. I stopped listening to the whispers in my gut and let my emotions take over. I decided to make it *get* better, for him, even if it meant bending the truth."

I can feel Audrey's stare. I look over and see she's arching an eyebrow.

"Okay, lying," I add. "I tried to right a lie with another lie, and that's how all of this started. With a lie. And if I'd told the truth, none of this would have happened. But, also, if I told the truth, none of this would have happened. So, I'm left with a personal dilemma: What is the better way of dealing with this tragedy? To let it disappear, to let the boy I knew vanish into the lie of a father who refused to understand his son? Or to lie to myself and all of you, to retool this story into another one with a lesson for an ending? They're both built on lies, but at least one of them got us here tonight. Not to this award but here, celebrating Christopher's life, for who he really was. And hopefully, shedding a light on just how dangerous it is not to accept your kids unconditionally.

"There is no other moral of the story here. And please—let me be clear—just because Christopher didn't kill himself, it doesn't mean there aren't still hundreds of gay teenagers every year who commit or attempt suicide. That problem is very real, and very urgent, and needs to be addressed by everyone. By making this lie I didn't mean to trivialize such an important topic but instead hoped to bring it the attention it deserves. I am not going to tie this speech up into a pretty bow and walk away with a lesson that makes all of us feel better about our own stupid decisions and mistakes. I'm just going to leave you with this: Christopher was a good guy. And he deserved better. And I guess I thought that's what I was trying to give him. But it all got out of hand and it's my fault and I'm sorry. But blame me, forget about me, but please . . . never forget about Christopher and all the other teens who face what he faced."

There's some awkward and scattered applause, but I don't care. I walk offstage right into Audrey's embrace.

# STILL NOW

THE HOTEL SUITE THE ORGANIZATION has so sweetly given me is beyond the nicest hotel room I've ever seen. It's so nice that it almost frightens me.

"Sweet mother of Jackie O, this place is stunning," Audrey says, her jaw dropping so much I'm worried she'll get a rug burn.

We basically ran away from the party before Harrison or my parents could catch us. I'm sure they're worried and that my phone is lighting up with multiple *where are you?* texts but for this moment I don't care. I'm in a fancy New York City hotel suite with my best friend, and for the first time in weeks, an enormous weight has been lifted off my tired shoulders.

"Why do gay people have such good taste?" Audrey says, admiring a particularly glamorous floor lamp.

"They don't always," I tell her.

To which she looks at me and purses her heavily lined lips before spreading them into a smile.

"True. Your room is almost historically ugly."

"All right," I say, "let's not get carried away."

"It's like, do you go out of your way to be tacky?" she continues.

"Hilarious!" I deadpan. She laughs.

"Darling! There's a minibar!" Audrey dances across the room toward the fridge in the kitchenette. "We're having champagne!"

Being underage aside, we have zero business having champagne.

"Isn't the whole point of champagne to toast something?" I ask.

Audrey is already digging through the fridge and pulling out the bottle of expensive-looking champagne.

"We *are* toasting to something. We're toasting to you!"

After the events of the past few months, this is simply ridiculous.

"Oh, come on," I tell her, but she won't hear it.

"You did something brave tonight," Audrey says, unfolding the aluminum foil wrapped around the cork.

"After months of doing something really, really bad," I correct her.

The faint sound of New York City traffic can be heard outside the window, reminding me just how far from home I am and what a strange journey I've made for myself.

"You did the speech, you apologized, you told the truth. Did you do a very, very bad thing? No. A stupid thing? Yes. An irrational thing? Probably. But you know what else you did? You got people listening and talking about something important. That's what matters," Audrey says, placing two champagne flutes on the coffee table in front of us. The skyline of New York City glitters behind the sheer curtain that can be operated by a remote control. "If I've learned anything from the hours upon hours I've spent watching old movies, it's that sometimes we mess up, but what matters is you fought. You tried. And in some totally screwed-up way, you even succeeded."

"I did, didn't I?" I say, sheepishly ashamed of my own self-praise. "I did it oh so stupidly. But I did something. I didn't just sit there like I've done my entire life. I stood up."

She pops open the bottle, the sound fierce as a bullet, the foamy booze spilling onto her skirt.

"Thank God this isn't red," Audrey says into the wet mark across her vintage skirt before pouring the wine into our two glasses. The carbonated bubbles rise farther and farther to the top before disappearing.

"To making mistakes but doing what you can to fix them," Audrey says, her glass raised.

"To fighting for what's right," I say, raising my glass, joining her. "And to Christopher, and trying to do what I think he'd want."

I feel my voice choke. It's been a long day of thinking about Christopher. I've thought about him so much it's almost as if he's been there the whole time. And by admitting this lie to the world, I am letting go of my own part of him. The part I've been holding on to this entire time. Standing there, for the first time, I actually accept just how gone he really is.

"To Christopher," Audrey toasts, holding my hand. "And to you. For doing what you could to honor his memory." She arches her eyebrows. "Even though it was freaking insane."

I slap her knee, wet from the champagne.

"KIDDING!" she shouts. "To you."

I smile. "To you."

We clink our glasses and take a long drink, the acidic bubbles burning down my throat.

"You know, by the time we leave here, every gay person in the world might hate me," I say, weighing the future for the first time.

"They very well might," Audrey agrees with a shrug, which isn't exactly what I was aiming for. "But you know what? One day they're going to realize you did what you thought was best."

I nod in agreement but am still unconvinced.

"Or they won't, and you'll spend the rest of your life as the kid who lied about a suicide," she adds. She wanders over to the balcony doors. "Wait, there's a balcony? What the hell are we doing inside?" Audrey shouts, unlatching the sliding door and pulling it open, the whirling sounds of New York City pouring in, rattling the calm room awake.

"What floor is this?" I ask. I haven't been paying attention.

"Twenty, I think?" she says, staring down at the lit-up city below. "Wow. Look at that. THAT is what I call determination."

She's staring down a few feet, on the wall beside our balcony. I crane my head to see, unsuccessfully.

"What?"

"That ladybug," she says. "I mean, the thing must have climbed all the way up here, right?"

I look, and she's right.

*Who doesn't like a ladybug?* Christopher asked, once upon a time. Over frozen yogurt. With the entire world ahead of us. With the promise of making it better for each other. The future. And it's stupid, and you should absolutely roll your eyes and tweet something snarky about it, because I probably will, but this is the moment I know that I'll never be able to forgive myself if I don't apologize to one more person.

# THE DAY AFTER NOW

REVEREND ANDERSON IS SET TO speak at the annual Christmas Eve concert organized by all the local churches in Winston-Salem. This is, needless to say, not the type of event my mom or I would normally be a part of, but after everything that's happened in New York I know this will be the best way to speak face-to-face with Christopher's mom.

We wait outside the church as the crowds gather and file into the city auditorium. I start sweating with nerves underneath my wool cardigan as families full of holiday cheer pass all around us. I've never been much of a Christmas person, but the energy and good spirits are palpable and impossible to ignore.

"Are you all right?" Mom asks, seeing my stressed expression. I nod, looking around, hoping to spot Angela without the reverend, who I assume will already be backstage preparing his lecture on how Santa Claus is actually the devil.

"There she is," Mom says quietly.

Christopher's mom is standing alone, looking timid, the past few heartbreaking months written across her face and frail body. What, I wonder, is going through her head? As she gets closer I wonder how odd it must be to begin your first Christmas without your only child. Had she already purchased him Christmas presents and hidden them under the bed for December? Will she hang his stocking? Will they put the Christmas ornaments every kid makes at school on their tree?

"Hello," Mom says, like someone defusing a bomb, as Christopher's mom passes by us before stopping in her tracks.

Christopher's mom nods, her mouth too clenched to speak.

"How are you?" I ask, the simplicity of the question seeming so out of place for what we're feeling.

The crowd around us laughs and gossips and hugs and exudes all the cheerfulness unique to the holidays.

Christopher's mom exhales a long breath I hadn't seen her take in, staring down at her black shoes.

"I'm sorry," I say, the words popping out. "I'm so sorry."

Christopher's mom steps closer to me and looks me directly in the eye. I wonder what she'll say. Will she slap me? Forgive me? Say something cruel? I deserve any and/or all of it.

But instead she wraps her arms around me, pulling me into her. I am struck, at first, by how she smells a bit like Christopher. The same detergent. Or shampoo. Or genetics. Or maybe a combination of the three.

She stays, holding me, for a while. I look up at my mother and wish Christopher were here to see this strange scene unfolding.

"Thank you for loving my son," she says into my shoulder, her breath hot and a little stale from nerves and coffee. "Thank you for doing what we couldn't do."

She pulls away and looks at me, squeezing my arms, her eyes red and puffy.

"I don't know why I went along with it all for so long. Why I allowed Jim to treat him so horribly. Why? Why didn't I do something? Why didn't I fight for him like you?" With every word she speaks, her voice gets more and more frantic.

"It's okay," I say out of habit . . . but is it? Should someone be forgiven for making their child's life miserable?

"After I saw that photo of you two, at that dance, I couldn't take it. He looked so happy. I was his mother and I had never seen him smile like that. Isn't that awful? I'd never seen him smile so happily." She shakes her head. "And I said, 'Jim, what are we doing?' And he said we're standing up for God. I said, 'But what about standing up for our son?' He didn't have an answer. All that fighting and never once for our boy."

"We make mistakes, Angela," Mom says, stepping forward and taking her hand.

Christopher's mom nods, with a spirit not just broken but shattered. I am proud of her. Proud of Christopher. And proud of myself. For someone who has never done anything with his life, I feel like I have finally actually done something. Maybe it's selfish, but this moment alone tells me my lie has all been worth it. I fought for something, for someone I loved, and there aren't many things one can do that are as important as that. Sometimes the fight becomes so loud, and you forget what you're fighting for. But like Audrey said, you have to fight fair, or what's the point of fighting at all? I fought for Christopher in my own screwed-up way. But I did something. For the first time in my life, I didn't just sit there. And despite breaking the rules, I made my point, and for the first time ever, maybe in my entire lifetime, I feel borderline accomplished.

Staring up at the cold night sky, I say a quiet good-bye to Christopher, and us, and our future, and promise to try to *make* it get better. The world doesn't change just by complaining about it online. You have to fight. And I'm going to keep doing so. For him and all the other people out there like him whose voices are sometimes never heard. And I hope you will too.

# acknowledgments

This book wouldn't exist without my remarkable and lovely editor, David Levithan. I also owe a great deal of gratitude to my awesome team: Brandi Bowles, Kara Baker, and Cullen Conly. Same goes to my parents, Scott and Nancy. I am really lucky to be surrounded by supportive and innovative queer voices who remind me to keep going, even when the clouds seem too dark, so thank you to all those folks who know who they are. And lastly, to Augie Prew, my boyfriend and best friend and my absolute favorite person to watch TV with.

# about the author

**Jeffery Self** is a writer, actor, and vlogger. If his face is familiar, it may be because he's appeared in numerous films and television shows, including *30 Rock*, *Desperate Housewives*, and *Search Party*. Or you're one of the millions of people who've viewed him on YouTube. Or you read *Drag Teen*, his first YA novel, which was an ALA Best Fiction for Young Adults recipient.

For more about Jeffery, check him out on Twitter at @JefferySelf and online at jefferyself.tumblr.com and www.youtube.com/user/JefferySelf.